A note from Rosalie Warren . . .

I wrote *Coping with Chloe* because I am fascinated by the mystery of twins, the way the human brain works and how we come to terms with losing someone very close to us. I was thinking about these things when the character of Anna appeared and started talking.

Anna's experiences are all very real to her. How you interpret her story is entirely up to you.

Coping
with
Chloe

ROSALIE WARREN

COPING WITH CHLOE

ISBN: 978-1-907912-02-3

Published in Great Britain by Phoenix Yard Books Ltd

This edition published 2011

Phoenix Yard Books
Phoenix Yard
65 King's Cross Road
London
WC1X 9LW

1 3 5 7 9 10 8 6 4 2

Set in Garamond MT Std 13.5/19 pt
Typeset by Palimpsest Book Production Limited, Falkirk, Stirlingshire

Printed in Great Britain by the CPI Group

A CIP catalogue record for this book is available from the British Library

www.phoenixyardbooks.com

To Dan and Em, with love

Chapter 1

I'm getting worried about Mum.

Yesterday she was worse than ever. You should have seen her when Chloe got Garfie to do his beg-for-a-biscuit trick. The way her face went white, you'd think she'd seen a ghost – and then she dropped the fruit bowl.

Garfie has been doing his tricks for years and Mum has never reacted like that before. Why would she?

Garfie is our golden Labrador. Actually he's more Chloe's dog than mine. He made up his mind about that the day he came to live with us on our eighth birthday, nearly five years ago. It upset me at the time but I've kind of got used to it.

Garfie has never, ever done a single trick for me, and it's always Chloe he rushes up to when we get home from school. Or, I should say, it always was.

Mum is just Mum – except that recently she hasn't been herself at all. Not since Chloe . . . Well, I'll tell you more about that soon.

Dad lives with his girlfriend Nikki on the other side of the park. Mum hates Nikki, and Chloe and I pretend to, for Mum's sake.

Anyway, Mum came in just as Garfie was up on his hind legs, about to topple over. Mum made a funny gulping noise and dropped the bowl. Then, as the apples and oranges rolled across the carpet, she screamed – a real horror-movie shriek. It made my neck prickle to hear her. Poor Garfie must have wondered what he'd done wrong.

I thought of the old days, when Mum wasn't afraid of anything. Even Dad was happy for her to be the one in charge. We didn't mind her being bossy, because she was so interested in everything we did. When Chloe and I came home from school and told her things, she would listen properly, with the right kind of expression on her face – sympathetic or happy, proud of us or whatever.

As I stroked Garfie's neck to comfort him, Mum picked up the fruit from the floor. Then she sort of collapsed on the sofa and said, "Sorry, Anna. I'm a bundle of nerves these days."

"It's OK," I said, staring at her and trying to work out what it was about her that had changed so much. Mum is tall and graceful and always looks good, even around the house. Or she used to. She still puts on her smart clothes for work, but she never bothers with make-up or jewellery any more. And at home she often wears the same top in the evenings for a week or more without washing it (yuk).

Speaking of tall and graceful, Chloe got the tall gene from Mum, though not the graceful one. She is a couple of centimetres taller than me and her hair is a lovely glowing ginger, whereas mine is like Mum's, a dull reddish brown that Mum calls auburn. Chloe also has Mum's green eyes, while I've inherited Dad's grey ones.

As I kissed her goodnight downstairs, Mum said, "It's just me and you and Garfie now, kid. We three will have to stick together."

I reminded her about my sister. "There's Chloe, too."

Mum burst into tears. I pushed the tissue box into her hands and fled up to my room.

At teatime today I told Mum about the poetry competition. "Miss Tough's organising it. We have to write a poem of twenty lines or less. It can be about anything we like."

Miss Tough is our English teacher and also our form tutor.

Mum looked up from her poached eggs on toast. I could see her making a big effort to listen. Sometimes I wonder if it would be better not to speak to her at all.

"I didn't know you wrote poetry," she said.

"I haven't, before. But I thought I'd have a go."

Mum didn't answer so I went on, "I thought I might write a poem about Garfie."

"That's a good idea."

She didn't mean it, not really. I could see that she didn't care.

"Unless you can think of something better," I said.

"No, I can't think of anything. Of course, Chloe was always the imaginative one."

4

I hate it when Mum says things like that. I wanted to tell her that Chloe was going to enter the competition as well, but I knew it would upset her.

I said, "Well, there's no reason why I can't have a go. Miss Tough told me I should."

"Nice woman, Miss Tough," said Mum. I knew she was thinking about all the meetings they'd had together since last October. They'd mainly talked about me – about whether I should be put into a different class or even sent to another school.

It was Mrs Furze who had put her foot down about that. "Keep things as much the same as you can," I heard her tell Mum.

"I'll try, but it's not easy," Mum replied.

"I know," said Mrs Furze. "But we must do our best."

In my room after tea, I spent ages trying to write a poem. Mum is right; Chloe is the imaginative one. I'd hoped my twin might give me some ideas, but she was off on one of her little trips. Probably in the garden, pulling petals off the flowers, the way we used to do when we were little.

Maybe Garfie wasn't a good subject for a poem. I got as far as:

> *We have a golden Labrador,*
> *His name is Garfie too.*
> *He's big and strong and bouncy,*
> *And his faults are very few.*

I wasn't happy with it. For one thing, Miss Tough had said not to worry about making it rhyme, but I felt I had to. If it didn't rhyme, what made it a poem? The "too" in the second line wasn't right, either, but I couldn't think of another word to fit.

I wished Garfie was our second Labrador. Granny Henderson calls her cat Topsy Two because she had a first Topsy, who died. "Garfie Two" would make my poem so much better.

Then I felt a sharp stab in my stomach (I think that's where my conscience lives). Was I really wishing that Garfie would die, so we could get another dog and call him Garfie Two? I told myself not to be stupid, but the bad feeling wouldn't go away.

Speaking of Granny Henderson – I miss her. She

lives miles away, at the seaside, and I haven't seen her since Dad left home.

Mum is not the only one who gets through the tissues these days. I have a big pile of used ones under my bed.

Chapter 2

*T*hings got even more complicated today. There's a new boy in our form group – Joe Medway. He turned up late this morning, when we were in the middle of a discussion with Miss Tough about the new school uniform. Lisa Major was sounding off about how green was her worst colour and if they tried to make us wear it she would never come to school again (I wish!).

My stomach started fizzing when Miss Tough said, "Ah, Joe. Welcome to our group. Find yourself a seat. We'll do some introductions in a minute," and I realised he was here to stay.

Joe has dark curly hair, huge brown eyes with long

lashes, and a big smile. Daydream material. Of course, every girl in the class started fancying him in the first few seconds. Every girl except Kelly Gascoigne, at least. Kelly may well have fancied him, but you'd never know because she never says a word.

We girls all started buzzing like a hive of bees and we didn't care about the new uniform any more. Even Lisa stopped yakking and stared at Joe, her mouth hanging open.

Usually I don't even try my luck with the better-looking boys. I'm not exactly ugly but in our class we have three bitchy bimboes who don't give anyone else a chance. Lisa Major is the main one – and she's a bully.

Joe found himself a seat near the back, between Ahmed Khan and William Grey. He kept his eyes down, not looking at any of the girls, not even Lisa, who was fluttering her lashes like she'd got a fly in her eye.

Maybe Joe was shy?

He raised his head and looked round the room just once, while Miss Tough was talking about our homework timetable. He caught my eye and I felt my cheeks turn warm and red. I tried to smile – an ordinary, welcoming smile. I'm not sure how it came out, but he gave a weird twisted grin back at me.

That's when I started liking him. It was a sort of "Help. Save me from these people!" expression, not what you'd expect from a boy who looked like Joe.

Miss Tough asked if I would look after him on his first day – show him around the school, make sure he got to the right classes and so on. I couldn't believe my luck, especially when I saw Lisa's face.

Joe gave me another smile. Was he pleased that I was the one who was going to show him round or was he trying to hide his embarrassment at being shown around by a girl? I suppose it was a bit weird when you think about it. You'd think Miss Tough would have asked another boy.

I could so easily have wrecked things. If Joe had been a different kind of boy, that's probably what would have happened. But when I said to him, on our way to geography, "This is my twin sister, Chloe," he only let himself look puzzled for a few seconds before saying, "Hi there, Chloe."

I thought I'd better explain. I didn't want him to

think I was a headcase. Luckily we were outside, crossing the playground, and no one else was in earshot.

"Chloe and I share a body," I said. "We're twins."

Joe skidded to a stop and stared at me, head on one side as though he was trying to work this out. I was half-expecting him to turn and run, but he didn't.

I went on, "Chloe lost her body a few months ago. That's why she shares mine now." My stomach was gurgling and my legs had gone all weak.

Joe's eyes opened wide. "Wow! That's unusual."

I set off again, walking slowly, and he kept pace. "No one understands," I said. "Miss Tough does her best, but all the others ignore Chloe. It's like she doesn't exist anymore and it really hurts her feelings."

Joe screwed up his face as if he was thinking. "So does she have a voice of her own?" he asked, so quietly I could hardly make out the words.

"Of course I do," said Chloe.

It was lovely to hear her join in. Often, these days, she just sulks quietly, which isn't surprising when you think about it. Anyone would sulk if they were ignored all the time.

"Anna and Chloe . . ." Joe said slowly. "Two for the price of one."

"That makes us sound like bottles of shampoo."

"Sorry." He'd speeded up again and we had almost reached the science block. Lisa and her friends were hanging about outside – three pairs of eyes on us.

"Chloe's voice is a bit different from yours," Joe said. "Not so loud, maybe?"

He'd noticed! He *recognised* Chloe – saw that we were different people. I felt like skipping, in full view of Lisa and the others. "That's right. She's more shy than me."

Joe smiled his lovely smile, showing off the dimples in his cheeks and chin. "Do I have to choose, or can I be friends with both of you?"

I waited for Chloe to answer. "With both of us. That'd be great."

I smiled too, though I had an uneasy feeling. But what was the alternative? It wouldn't be fair to ask Joe to choose between Chloe and me at this stage and, what's more, I knew I wouldn't be happy either way. If he chose Chloe . . . well, that would be horrible. And if he chose me, I'd feel guilty.

You can't win, sometimes, with a twin. Especially when you're both crammed into the same body.

*

Joe got excited when he saw the swimming pool and said he was training for the county junior butterfly team.

"Will you teach me to swim butterfly?" I asked.

"Sure. It's easy."

"I've tried lots of times but I can't get my arms high enough over my head."

"It's all about timing," said Joe. "And getting a strong thrust with your legs. I'll show you."

"Brilliant," Chloe and I said together. This sometimes happens, and makes us feel a bit silly. But of course no one ever notices these days.

Joe, however, gave a little giggle. Had he really heard Chloe and me speak at the same time? If so, this boy was something special.

I could feel Chloe's brain going all gooey as we walked back to the main block and headed for maths. Mine was pretty much the same, though I had the feeling, even stronger now, that things could get complicated.

Trouble might well be brewing, but it was an exciting kind of trouble that made me tingle from head to foot.

Chapter 3

"*I* can't do this stuff!"

It was Joe's third day at our school and I'd got to know him well enough by now to see that he was almost in tears.

I didn't let on that I knew, though. I just said, "I know the feeling. With me, it's geography that makes me feel stupid."

Joe wasn't really listening and he gave another groan.

I asked, "Want a bit of help?"

"OK."

I took a quick glance round the classroom. Miss Tough was over the other side, saying something to

Kelly Gascoigne. I leaned over Joe's exercise book to see what he'd done. His handwriting was so bad I could hardly make out a word. The page was speckled with squirts and blotches from his cheap, half-broken biro.

"See what I mean?" he said.

I was about to answer when I spotted a movement from Miss Tough out of the corner of my eye. "Shh," I said. "She's looking. I'll help you later. See you by the vending machine at break."

But towards the end of the lesson, Miss Tough came over to Joe and looked at his work. "Have you ever been tested for dyslexia?" she asked.

Joe nodded his head. "At my primary school they told me I had it. But my last school said I'd grown out of it and I was OK now."

"I think we should have you tested again," said Miss Tough. Her voice was gentle, as it usually was, except when dealing with Lisa and her friends. "Don't worry, Joe. If you are dyslexic, you'll be able to get extra help, as well as more time in exams, that sort of thing."

I kind of felt Joe relax as she said this. I could

almost see his worries bubbling out of his head and floating up towards the ceiling.

At break, I said, "Do you still want a hand with your essay?"

"It's OK, Anna. Thanks, anyway, but Miss Tough's going to help me. She's brilliant."

I liked Miss Tough even more after this. She is one of those adults you feel must have made the wrong decision at some stage in her life, because she's far too nice to be a teacher. Her first name is Alice and she told us once that her mother named her after *Alice in Wonderland*. That made me jealous – I would *so* love to be named after a character in a book.

I said that to Mum and she said, "Be thankful Dad and I didn't call you Bilbo Baggins."

Ages ago, I asked Miss Tough if there were any books with Annas in them and she told me about a book called *Anna Karenina*, by a Russian author named Tolstoy. I decided to pretend (at least to myself) that I was named after her, until clever-clogs Phoebe Pointer told me that Anna Karenina came to a sticky end.

That put paid to that little daydream. Our parents obviously got our names the wrong way round.

Not that I'd fancy falling down a rabbit hole, either.

Last October, when Chloe and I had only been back at school for a week or so after . . . well, after *it* happened, Miss Tough asked us to write an imaginative story in class.

When she read what was in my notebook, she said, "This is more like Chloe's style than yours, Anna."

My best friend, Lennie, who was sitting next to me, gave a gasp. I expect it was because Miss Tough had said Chloe's name. Everyone seemed to have decided that the word "Chloe" was banned. At home, if I said it, Mum went doolally and Dad, who was still living with us then, changed the subject straightaway. Our neighbours, Mr and Mrs Stevens, turned bright red when I told them that Chloe was sharing my body. I could see they thought I was mad, and I stopped telling most people after that.

Anyway, I said to Miss Tough, "That's because Chloe wrote it," and Lennie gave a louder gasp that was almost a choke.

The others had started to listen in and there was a hum of excitement in the room.

Miss Tough just said, "Ah, I see," and moved on to something else.

At the end of the lesson she asked me to stay behind a minute.

She read Chloe's story again, more slowly this time. When she got to the end, she said, "This is very good."

I beamed with pride for my sister and she beamed with pride for herself. It makes things a lot easier when we want to make the same expression at the same time.

"A very exciting and well-written story," Miss Tough went on.

"Thank you," said Chloe, finding her voice at last.

Miss Tough hesitated for a few seconds. "Did you write a story too, Anna?" she asked.

"Not yet," I said. "Mine's still inside my head. I'll do it for homework."

"That would be good," said Miss Tough. She is very pretty, with long dark hair that she puts in an old-fashioned ponytail. Her eyes are greyish-green and she has a mischievous smile.

"I'll hand it in on Thursday," I said, wishing I could stay longer, not wanting to go to history with Mr Crewe. But there was a new class lining up outside the English and Media Studies door.

Miss Tough half got up from her chair, then changed her mind and sat back down. "Are you happy with Chloe writing stories, Anna?" she asked.

"Yes. I don't mind, if that's what she wants to do."

Miss Tough looked a bit awkward and a faint blush appeared on her cheek. "I just meant . . . the way things are now."

"You mean now that Chloe and I are sharing a body?"

"Yes. That's what I meant. Are you happy with it – with the whole thing?"

I thought for a few seconds. "It's a bit of a nuisance in some ways, but I'm getting used to it. We both are."

"Good."

I thought for a minute she was going to touch my hand. That would have been embarrassing, though quite nice in a way.

I said, "The worst thing about it is that no one understands."

Miss Tough gave a big sigh. "I can see it might be difficult." Then she went quiet again.

I started to feel uncomfortable. "I'd better go now. I've got history."

"Yes, of course. Tell Mr Crewe I kept you back."

"OK."

No way was I going to do that. The rest of my class would think I'd been crying on Miss Tough or something. I decided to tell them I'd stopped off in the toilets for a smoke. No one would believe me but it would keep them guessing.

A week or two after that, Lennie decided that she didn't want to be my friend any more. Jessica, my second-best friend, did the same thing a few days later. Around the same time, Dad left us to move in with Nikki from his work, in her posh flat with the spanking new kitchen and huge TV. Nikki is twenty-seven, skinny as a model and wears the shortest skirts you've ever seen and designer shoes with five-inch platform heels.

It wasn't a good time, though I had no idea, back then, how much worse things were going to get.

Chapter 4

Chloe has rescued me twice so far this week. In our geography test, Miss Brown asked us for the capital of Peru and my mind went completely blank. Maybe it was because Joe was sitting next to me again. He wasn't doing anything to distract me, just being his usual gorgeous self. He would put anyone off their geography test.

Anyway, the place in my head where I keep things like capital cities was all closed up, but right there in *her* usual place, bang-centre, was Chloe. She was always a bit of a swot. In fact, the morning of the accident I was rushing to get to school to finish my French, which I should have done the night before. Chloe had done hers, of course.

"Fancy forgetting the capital of Peru," she said now. "What'll you give me if I tell you?"

"Anything," I whispered back. I hadn't meant to speak out loud – I don't need to, for Chloe to hear me. But I must have made some kind of noise because Joe looked up.

I gave a little cough and blew my nose.

"Well?" asked my twin.

"Custard for dinner?" I suggested. Chloe loves custard on her pudding and I hate it. I could force myself to eat it, though, if it meant being saved from failure in the geography test.

"OK," she said. "The capital of Peru is Lima."

Lima, of course. I scribbled it down, just in time, before Miss Brown moved on to the next question.

Unfortunately, though, Chloe never helps out when I'm doing maths. It was always her worst subject and things haven't changed a bit.

*

The second time Chloe helped me was much worse – or rather it would have been, if she hadn't stepped in. As often happens, the person behind the trouble was Lisa Major. Mr Crewe, our history teacher, had put us in groups to work on a project about Leeberdale Castle, which is a few miles down the road towards Kettleby.

Unfortunately, he'd put me in the same group as Lisa. I didn't expect her to do much work – I just hoped she wouldn't mess things up for the rest of us. The good thing was that Joe was also in my group.

We agreed among ourselves who would do what and then we each did some work on our own, looking things up in books and on the Internet. Unlucky people like Joe and me, who don't have computers at home, had to do their research in the library at lunchtime. For the millionth time, I pestered Mum for a computer. All she said was, "It's your dad's fault for taking it with him when he left. You'll have to talk to him about it."

Some hope of doing that, when I hardly ever see him.

Joe and I met up in the library every lunchtime for

a week. "You'll need to help me with my sentences," he said on the first day. "If that's OK?"

"Of course it is," I said, glad to have a reason to spend more time with him.

I scribbled away and managed, in the end, to produce five whole pages. Since I was group coordinator, everyone had to hand in their work to me. That meant I had to pester some of them for three days to get them to give me anything at all.

"Sorry, that's the best I could do," said Joe on the last day, handing me a single sheet.

I knew he'd put in a lot of effort, so I said, "Well done," and put his paper on the pile. It was all going to go onto the computer, so I would have a try, later on, at working out what he'd meant to say and rewriting it.

Then Lisa pushed a bundle of paper into my face. "Here, Swottybot," she said. "Or should that be Snottybot?"

Is Lisa ever going to grow up?

I was surprised, though – she'd written more than anyone. Very unusual for Lisa, even if she does have a laptop at home.

"I hate being group coordinator," I said to Joe as we sat on the wall behind the kitchens one break. "I'm worried our group will get a bad mark."

"Maybe I can help," he said. "I'm not much good at the actual writing, but if you want a hand with sorting out everyone's stuff . . ."

My heart started thumping away in excitement. "Yes, please!"

He grinned. "OK. Tomorrow lunchtime? Maybe we can find somewhere quiet to meet up? Not the library, because we can't talk properly there."

I had a feeling he wasn't just saying it out of kindness. It was beginning to look as if – just possibly – the feelings weren't all on my side. Maybe Joe was pleased to have an excuse to spend more time with me . . . and with Chloe too, of course.

We found ourselves a corner of the art room, which someone had forgotten to lock between lessons. It was full of self-portraits done by the third years, and we spent a few minutes laughing at the piggy noses and bum-shaped chins. Not that I could have done any better, nor Joe, nor most other people we knew.

Kelly Gascoigne is the only person in our class who can really draw.

As we started to look through it all, we saw that most of the project stuff was OK. We had to decide what should go in each chapter and I'd volunteered to write an introduction, though I was beginning to wish I hadn't.

In the old days, Mum or Dad would have given me good advice. But when I told Mum about the history project she just said, "That sounds good," and went back to her daydream.

I tried phoning Dad, but he was away on a work trip and I got Nikki, who said, "Hello Anna, how are *you* today?" in a marmaladey voice that made me want to throw up.

Phoebe Pointer had done a good description of a soldier in the Middle Ages. She went through his day, starting with what he had for breakfast and so on. Joe's effort was full of spelling mistakes, bad punctuation, run-on sentences and some words I couldn't make out at all. It didn't matter though, because he was beside me to explain what he'd meant.

Ahmed Khan had done some good drawings of

the castle to go with his essay. Jemima Kerr had taken photos and Lennie had told the story of the Leeberdale ghost (a happy kitchen maid who sings ballads to herself).

As I was going through all this, Joe was reading Lisa's contribution – or trying to. "Can't tell what she's on about," he said.

I looked across at where he'd spread Lisa's work out on one of the art tables (too late, I realised there was red powder paint spilt there and some of the work had got a bit smeared with it). Except for the red paint, Lisa's stuff looked amazing. There was eleven pages of it, all set out in a fancy font.

"This isn't like Lisa," I said, starting to read.

It was even harder to understand than Joe's, but for a different reason. I didn't know what half the words meant. The sentences were long and complicated and I got to the end of the first page without having a clue what it was about. Churches? Religion? Saints?

"I'll have to put it in as it is," I said. "I don't fancy talking to Lisa about it."

I suppose I should have been suspicious, but as usual I was distracted by Joe, as well as busy thinking about how to put everything together. I went to sleep that night with it all whizzing round inside my head.

In the middle of the night, Chloe's voice woke me up. "She's a cheat!"

"What?" I was too sleepy to remember that Chloe didn't have a body any more. I put the light on and leaned over the edge of my bed to look at her in the bottom bunk. When I saw the bare mattress, I got one of those horrible jolts, like when Dad's car bumps over a pothole in the road.

"Chloe . . ." I called out.

"Shh," she said. "You'll wake Mum up. Listen a minute. D'you really think Lisa wrote that stuff herself?"

Something clicked in my head. The mass of text, the long words, the complicated sentences . . .

"Use your brain, Anna," said Chloe.

"So who did write it?" I was still half asleep, fuzzy-headed and confused.

"It's all copied from the Web. Can't you tell? Lisa Major couldn't write that stuff in a million years. She can't even string three words together on her own."

It made perfect sense. Why hadn't I seen it for myself?

"What shall I do?" I said. "If we hand it in, Mr Crewe will take marks off us for cheating."

Chloe made a hissing sound through her teeth. "Tell Lisa, of course, that you've found her out. Make her do it again in her own words."

I don't remember any more after that. I suppose I must have gone back to sleep.

Next morning, my conversation with Chloe felt like a dream. At school I looked through Lisa's pages again, half-expecting them to be OK. But no, the strange words and the long sentences – some of them going on for a whole paragraph – were still there.

I challenged Lisa: "Do you realise you nearly got our group into big trouble?"

I could tell she knew what I meant, though she put on a silly face and said, "What's the matter with you today, Anna FussBag?"

"Write it again in your own words or I'll tell on you."

Lisa turned bright red and opened her mouth to argue with me.

Then Chloe said in a firm voice, "Just do it, Lisa."

Lisa's mouth dropped open even further. She looked at me as though I'd changed into a monster – or, perhaps, into my sister? It was the first time I'd ever seen her look frightened. She gave her friend Poppy a quick glance and ran off.

At break, Joe said, "Well done, Chloe."

Chloe pushed my mouth into a smile.

Lisa rewrote her piece on saints and gave it to me the next day without saying a word. It wasn't very good, but our group still got the second highest mark.

Joe said to me, "Chloe is quieter than you, but she's quite scary when she puts her mind to it."

Chloe, my timid twin, scary? I laughed out loud at the thought.

That night, I went to bed feeling happier than I'd done for ages. My new friendship with Joe was the first good thing to happen since before Chloe lost her body.

Of course, Chloe was a bit of a worry. What would she do if Joe and I started going out together? Would she get jealous? Would she even try to steal him from me?

No, I told myself, Chloe would never do that. She wasn't the kind of sister who would boyfriend-steal. She'd do her best to keep out of our way; perhaps she would go off to her secret hiding place when Joe and I were together.

Chloe was my wonderful twin – always on my side. Look at the way she'd helped me with the geography test and then with Lisa's cheating.

There was really nothing to worry about.

Chapter 5

A few days after the history project fiasco, I saw Lisa Major coming on really strong to Joe at break, twirling round and round so her skirt went up and showed lots of leg. But Joe wasn't interested. He looked round for someone to rescue him and there I was, ready and waiting.

He gave a big grin when he saw me, and Lisa flounced off in disgust.

"Still want to learn the butterfly?" he asked.

"Course I do."

"How about tomorrow?"

The pool is open to the public after school two days a week, with special reduced prices for students.

"Sounds good," I said, my stomach going all frothy with excitement.

Chloe butted in. "Has Mum mended your swimming costume yet?"

The strap had almost gone and I'd had to use a safety-pin last week to keep it in place. I'd worried all through the session that someone would notice, but fortunately everyone's eyes were on Lisa Major – or on Joe.

"I'll ask her again this evening," I said.

But Mum was in one of her weepy moods. She'd been watching *EastEnders* and something in it had set her off.

"I don't know why you watch that stuff," I said, the way Dad used to.

"Makes me feel a bit better." She pulled another tissue out of the box and blew her nose.

"Any chance you could mend my swimming costume?" I asked.

She gave her nose an even noisier blow. "What did you say, Anna?"

"My swimming costume – the strap's gone . . . please . . ."

"Oh, Anna. You're nearly thirteen – can't you do it yourself?"

I suppose she was right – I was old enough to mend my own strap. But I've never been able to sew. Back in the old days, when Chloe still had her body, Mum would have got out her sewing box and done it straightaway.

For some reason it mattered much more than the baked beans we'd had for tea again (Mum couldn't be bothered cooking so I heated them up and made some toast). Sometimes I feel as though I'm not important to Mum any more, now that Chloe (so she thinks) isn't here.

And I was worried about that strap. If I cobbled it together with my horrible big stitches, it could easily come apart. If my swimming costume fell down while swimming with Joe, well, think of the embarrassment. And he'd probably never speak to me again.

Who, I wondered, could I ask to sew my strap back on?

Then I had a thought. Kelly! The only time I'd ever heard Kelly put more than a couple of words together was when she told us she'd won a prize in a sewing competition.

Hmm. Trouble was, I felt a bit guilty about asking her. She'd think I was being friendly, when really I was just using her. The trouble was, you see, I didn't really like Kelly – she wasn't my sort of person. Sadly for her, she didn't seem to be anyone's sort of person. The fact that she never said a word didn't help.

In some ways, Chloe is kinder than me and when she had her own body she used to be friendly to Kelly. For instance, she would offer to be her partner when we had to get into twos. I could tell that Chloe still wanted do this, but now that we only had one body between us, it meant that *I* would have to be Kelly's partner. I'd tried a few times but she drove me nuts, hanging around with her strange, miserable silence.

As I thought about asking Kelly to mend my swimming costume, Chloe butted in. "You're a creep." That was nice, coming from my twin. But I knew what she meant.

I *couldn't* back out of swimming with Joe, though – and I needed my costume mended, anyway, for next week's swimming class. There was only one thing for it — I'd have to ask Kelly and then go on being nice to her, at least for a while. If I didn't do that, Chloe would never let me hear the last of it.

You have to make sacrifices, when true love is calling.

There's something special about arranging to go swimming with a boy — it feels almost like a date. Especially as Joe's going to be giving me close attention, carefully watching all my arm and leg and body movements. Though I don't expect he'll be impressed by my swimming. I'm not very sporty, though I'm better than Chloe used to be.

The thing I'm best at is English. Joe is having trouble with most of his subjects, except maths, which he loves. I feel sorry for him in class a lot of the time. Some of the teachers are mean. Don't they know he's dyslexic? You'd think he was mixing up his letters just to annoy them, the way they go on.

Miss Tough isn't like that, of course, and neither is Miss Bunter, who teaches biology and can't spell herself. I don't mean she can't spell "herself", though she probably can't . . . Oh, forget it.

Miss Bunter is my second-favourite teacher in the school. She is very thin, which Dad thinks is hilarious. That's because his favourite book is *Billy Bunter of Greyfriars School* – and Billy Bunter was seriously overweight.

Anyway, I need to learn, as Miss Tough says, to "stay on topic".

I've promised Joe to teach him how to write in proper sentences, in return for him teaching me butterfly. I want to make sure he doesn't back out after the first session, when he sees how bad I am.

I went up to Kelly at break, trying to look friendly, but not too friendly, if you know what I mean. She was on her own at the snack table, choosing between an apple and a banana. Or maybe she was just trying to make the time go by. Break time must seem very long if you haven't got any friends.

"Hi, Kelly. I liked your picture," I said.

We'd just come from art and Kelly had produced an amazing picture of a stormy sea. Mr Bates said it was semi-abstract (I'm not sure what he meant but it was obvious from his funny little smile and the way his bald head went pink that he loved it) and had put it straight up on the wall.

Kelly looked round at me, her eyes wide open with surprise. "*Did* you?"

"It's lovely," I said. "Wish I could draw and paint."

I looked for Chloe in the centre of my head, wanting her to be pleased with me. So far I'd only been honest – surely she couldn't object to that. But my sister wasn't saying a word.

I was half-expecting Kelly to go silent on me, too, but she gave another smile. "I'd rather be good at other things than art," she said.

I didn't ask what. I had a feeling she meant making friends, stuff like that.

"Erm, Kelly, could you help me? I've got a broken cossie strap."

"Want me to sew it up for you?"

People were watching us now. I could see Lisa not far off, with Poppy and Kirsten beside her, waiting to pounce.

"Could you? I'd ask my mum but she won't . . . I mean, she's too busy."

"OK," said Kelly. After a pause, she asked, "Will you be my partner for drama tomorrow?"

I'm ashamed to say that I nearly said "no". I wanted Joe for a partner. Then I felt Chloe, deep inside my brain, nudging me.

"OK," I said.

Kelly gave me a big grin and offered me half her banana.

"What's a run-on sentence?" Joe asked me at break, on the day we were going for our swim. "Miss Tough tried to explain it but I didn't understand."

I glimpsed Lisa Major out of the corner of my eye, snooping on us. She hates it when I talk to Joe. I'm not sure how much it's that she likes him and how much she just hates the idea that a boy could like me better than her.

I pretended not to see her and said to Joe, "It's when you use a comma instead of a full stop."

He gave a little frown and scratched his cheek. "Do I know what a comma is?"

"Probably. Most people do." I glanced across at Lisa, but she was flailing her arms around now, probably imitating one of the teachers, making the little group around her squeal.

"I'm not most people," said Joe.

"OK. Well, a comma is a curly thing on the line, to show that you haven't finished what you're writing."

"Think I know what you mean."

"Look out for them next time you read something. Do you know what a full stop is?"

He grinned. "Course I do. You think I'm stupid or something?"

"No, just checking."

Oh no – Lisa was heading in our direction now.

"OK, where were we?" asked Joe.

"Well, like I said, a run-on sentence is where you use a comma instead of a full stop."

"How do you know?"

"How do I know what?"

Lisa, followed by Poppy and Kirsten, had almost reached us. Lisa's face had its usual mocking expression.

"How do you know which one you're supposed to use?" Joe asked.

That had me stumped. Perhaps being a teacher is

not so easy after all. "It all depends . . ." Go away, Lisa, I willed.

"Depends on what?"

Fortunately, at that moment the bell rang. Joe and I had different classes for the rest of the afternoon, so I said, "See you at the pool."

"OK. I'll be in the water."

"What if I get there first?"

"Then *you'll* be in the water. But you won't be." He grinned. "Girls take forever to get changed."

"I don't."

"OK then, race you. Last one in the water is a . . ."

Lisa was up close now and had heard these last few words. "Going swimming with Joe?" she asked.

"No business of yours."

"Nice, the way he feels sorry for you, Little Miss Lonely."

"I'm not lonely."

"Ignore her – walk off," Chloe was whispering, but I took no notice.

"I meant you're lonely because you've lost your twin," said Lisa.

"Shh," said Kirsten.

"Once Joe's seen you in your cossie, he won't be interested, that's for sure," said Lisa. "Think you can get a boy, with *your* body?"

Kirsten and Poppy collapsed in shrieks of laughter.

"Get lost, you three," said Chloe.

Lisa gave a little jump, like before, and backed away.

Maybe Joe was right – Chloe *was* becoming scary. I don't know how her voice must have sounded to Lisa – maybe almost like mine but not quite? However she did it, Chloe could certainly get rid of Lisa and Co., which I'd never managed to do.

Good. I needed someone like the newly brave Chloe on my side. Maybe she, Joe and I together could get the better of Lisa and her silly friends.

Chapter 6

*I*n spite of Chloe's victory over Lisa, I could tell all afternoon that my twin wasn't happy about something.

"What's the matter?" I asked her during a quiet moment in maths.

She didn't answer.

I suddenly thought – perhaps it's the swimming with Joe? Chloe has never been keen on swimming and, what's more, she has always been frightened of boys. I'm a bit scared of them myself, but you have to grit your teeth and speak to them anyway. That's what Mum says, or used to say, before *it* happened.

Maybe Chloe was afraid that the strap would break

again. I knew it wouldn't, because Kelly's stitches were neat and firm, a double row of them.

"Look, Chloe, it's me he's meeting, not you," I said, hoping that would make her feel better.

But it just seemed to make things worse, and she didn't speak again all afternoon. She refused to help me out in our French test and I got four out of ten.

I felt a bit better, though, when I found out that Lisa Major had only got three.

At the end of the day, I pushed my homework stuff into my bag and ran towards the changing rooms. I bumped into Kelly, probably on the way to art club, and she asked me where I was going.

"Nowhere," I said, not even slowing down.

I could feel Chloe's disapproval ticking away in my head as I got changed.

My strap was a bit tighter now it had been mended, and it dug into my left shoulder. I hoped it wouldn't cramp my butterfly style.

I was annoyed to find that Joe was already in the water. How had he managed that? Maybe remedial English had finished earlier than French.

He was pounding up and down the pool with a butterfly stroke that turned me into a quivering jelly. What a body. What power in those arms and shoulders! I knew I would never in a million years learn to swim like that. But it didn't matter – all I wanted was to be in the water with Joe.

I usually take my time getting used to the cold water, but I didn't want him to see me being a wimp so I jumped straight in and set off with my best front crawl.

The pool was almost empty. I knew it would soon fill up with parents who'd met their kids from the primary school next door and were bringing them for an after-school swim.

Joe did a neat somersault turn at the deep end and thundered back towards me. He didn't stop until he got to the shallows, though he must have seen me waiting.

"Hi, Anna," he said. "Told you I'd get in first."

"Never mind that," I said, noticing the way the water poured off his face, catching the light and making his skin glow silver. "I want you to teach me. Show me how to get my arms to go over my head."

46

"Like this," he said, showing me. He explained it in detail, much better than I'd managed to tell him about the run-on sentences. But however hard I tried, I couldn't get the hang of it.

"I've got the wrong sort of arms," I said after ten minutes or so, puffing and panting from the effort.

"It takes a lot of practice. I've been doing it since I was five."

"Five?" I hadn't learn to swim until I was nine, though I had no intention of admitting that to Joe.

"You've got a good crawl action," he said. "Nice and smooth. You breathe at the right times, which is more than most people do."

I gave a little shiver of pleasure.

"How's your breaststroke?" he asked, and for some reason I blushed. I hoped he hadn't noticed. If he had, he ignored it.

"Not too bad," I said. "Want to see?"

He swam alongside me, going at what for him was snail's pace. I did my best demonstration of breaststroke, remembering to give a good scissor-kick with my legs and a long glide before I pulled back with my arms and raised my head.

"Pretty good," he said as I got my breath back at the deep end. "If I were you, I'd stick to breaststroke and front crawl."

"But I want to swim butterfly like you."

The pool was filling up with tiny tots and their fussy parents and we'd be lucky to manage a couple more lengths before it became impossible to move. We gave up and chatted in a corner at the deep end, treading water near the steps and keeping an eye on the lifeguard, who sometimes complains when people use the pool to talk.

"My dad's a swimmer," Joe said. "He used to be in the British team."

"Wow! Was he in the Olympics?"

"No, he never got picked. Came close, though."

Suddenly I didn't feel so bad about my poor performance at the butterfly. "Does your dad still swim?" I asked.

"Don't know. Haven't heard from him for years."

This made me want to hug Joe, though I didn't, of course. I looked at his face but he seemed as cheerful as ever, as far as I could tell with his goggles over his eyes.

"It's better, in some ways," he said. "Dad and Mum didn't get on. But it'd be nice to know where he is. I hope he's OK."

"Have you got any brothers and sisters?" I asked.

"Just one brother, Karl. He's . . ." Joe pulled down his goggles and rubbed one of his eyes.

"He's what?"

"He moved away. He works . . . somewhere down south."

I knew Joe was lying, or at least hiding the truth. But it wasn't the right moment to ask any more.

I'd spotted a gap – a clear channel the whole length of the pool. "Come on," I said, and we set off, me at my fastest and Joe at – well, nothing like his fastest, but pretending to race me.

As I was getting changed afterwards, I looked for Chloe in her place inside my head. I was hoping she'd be in a better mood, that the swimming hadn't been as bad as she'd expected. But either she was in a sulk or she'd gone off on one of her little trips, or both.

I told Mum about the butterfly lesson as we ate our evening meal of ham salad. "Joe was great," I said.

49

"He's really helping me. Butterfly's good fun when you know what you're doing."

"Good," said Mum, a million miles away. She picked up the mustard jar and started to read the ingredients on the label. That tells you how interested she was in what I said.

I wished Dad was there to tease me about boyfriends, though I used to hate it when he did.

"Can I ask Joe round here after school one day?" I dropped Garfie a piece of ham under the table.

Mum must have felt him lunge for the ham. She said, "We haven't got money to waste, you know. Garfie has his own food."

"I know. It was just a little bit. *Can* I have Joe round, Mum, please?"

Mum put the jar of mustard down and actually looked at me for a second. "Can't you ask Leonora instead?"

"I'm not friends with Lennie now."

"Why not? She's a lovely girl."

"Just one of those things." I didn't tell Mum that Lennie had called me a weirdo and a psychopath and now had a new best friend, Grace Atkins. Mum has enough to deal with as it is.

But I kept on at her, and by the end of the meal she'd agreed to have Joe to tea one day next week. I felt my stomach leapfrog. It made up for the fact that Mum had forgotten to buy any cake and all we had to finish off with were a few stale biscuits.

Chapter 7

Well, it's happened. Joe has been to our house – and it was a complete disaster.

Things started off quite well. Joe fell in love with Garfie at first sight, the way everyone always does. And Mum was nice enough at first. She gave Joe a big, welcoming grin that reminded me of the way she used to look.

When she'd gone into the kitchen to make the lasagne (or so I thought), Chloe spoke up. "Would you like to see Garfie's trick?" she asked Joe.

"Course I would, Chloe," said Joe.

That gave me a warm feeling inside. I love it when Joe recognises that it's Chloe speaking, not me. He sometimes gets it wrong, but not very often. Maybe it helps that he didn't know my sister before *it* happened. Or maybe Joe is just a special kind of person.

Chloe picked up a banana from the fruit bowl, peeled it and broke a piece off with my left hand. It's taken some getting used to, Chloe being left-handed. She always was left-handed, of course, though I never thought about it much when she had hands of her own. But now that we share a body, it feels weird the way she uses my – or rather *our* – left hand.

"Here, Garfie," said Chloe.

Garfie lumbered towards us, all excited, as he always is when anyone promises him food.

"Here boy, come on, get the banana," Chloe said.

Once Garfie had caught a whiff of it (he loves banana, though it sometimes makes him sick), Chloe raised our hand higher and we scrambled to our feet so that Garfie had to sit up on his hind legs – up, up, up until he was near to toppling-over point.

He made a last stretch and Chloe finally gave in. Garfie's jaw closed on the banana and he sank back down into a rolled-up rug of golden fur.

Joe was grinning. "That's amazing, Chloe," he said.

"Thanks," said Chloe. "I taught him when he was a pup. He won't do it for Anna."

"Is that right?" Joe asked.

I felt myself blush. "'Fraid so," I said. "Right from the start, Garfie would only do tricks for Chloe."

"We wanted a puppy each for our eighth birthday," Chloe explained. "But Dad said if we were having two dogs they'd have to be small ones – ones that would stay small."

"But we wanted a golden Labrador," I said. "Nothing else would do. So we agreed to share."

"We thought the puppy would love us both the same," said Chloe. "But the trouble was, Garfie met me first. We were supposed to go with Dad in the car to pick him up, but Anna had a bad tummy . . ."

". . . which turned out to be appendicitis," I went on. "So I was in hospital for the whole of Garfie's first week with us."

"Bad timing, that," said Joe.

"It was. By the time I came home, Garfie had bonded with Chloe and there was no room for me. Nothing I could do about it."

I could see Joe thinking hard, wrinkling up his nose as he tried to make sense of it all.

"So, now that . . ." He paused, being careful to choose the right words. "Now that you two share a body – can Garfie still tell which of you is which?"

"Oh yes," I said. "Watch what happens if *I* try and get him to do the hind legs trick."

Garfie didn't do it, of course. He just sat there giving me that "I'm not stupid, you know" look.

Joe was sceptical. "Maybe he's not hungry after the banana," he said.

So we had to demonstrate with a doggie-chocolate button – something we only give Garfie very occasionally, as a treat. First I tried – nothing. Then Chloe had a go. I don't need to tell you the rest.

Joe finally believed us. "That's well cool," he said. Then he pulled a face at me. "Though it's a bit tough on Anna."

"I don't mind, I'm used to it," I said – and suddenly realised that I wasn't lying. I'd been saying it for years and not meaning it. But it made me happy, now, to see Garfie sit up and beg for Chloe, with Joe watching. I suppose it was because it proved to Joe, without any doubt, that Chloe was still here with us.

Mum called us through for tea and I knew straightaway, from the lack of delicious smells in the kitchen, that there was no lasagne. I tried hard to swallow the big wodge of disappointment and hunger in my throat. It was worse because I'd told Joe that Mum always made lasagne when I had friends to tea.

"Sorry," said Mum as we sat down at the dining table. "I got one of my headaches and I didn't feel up to it."

"Don't worry, Mrs Henderson. I love lettuce sandwiches," said Joe.

He must have been lying, out of politeness. Not many thirteen-year-old boys love lettuce sandwiches, do they? Maybe he didn't actually hate lettuce – or not as much as I do – but it hardly fills you up. The bread wasn't very nice, either – just ordinary white, sliced stuff, nothing like the delicious crusty loaves Dad used to make in his bread maker. I expect Nikki gets to eat those now.

But the lack of lasagne wasn't the worst thing. Mum, would you believe it, hardly said a word. I'd got used to her silences, but she might have made a bit more of an effort with my new friend. She could have asked Joe about his swimming, if nothing else.

I tried once or twice to get a conversation going, and so did Chloe. She asked Joe if he'd ever had a pet.

"No," he said. "I've never been allowed."

"We had to pester you and Dad for a long time, didn't we, Mum, to get a dog?" I said, but Mum was away in a daydream.

Chloe started to sulk at that point, so it was just Joe and me, awkwardly talking about pets, school and the butterfly.

What a family, I thought, suddenly ashamed of my mum and sister. I'd never felt like that before and it gave me a sharp stab of pain in my stomach.

When Joe had eventually had enough lettuce sandwiches (he must have munched his way through at least nine of the soggy things), Mum brought out the dessert. It was chocolate Swiss roll from the supermarket and actually it wasn't too bad, specially as she'd got Cornish ice cream to go with it.

As Joe tucked into his third helping, I thought of something different to ask him. "Are you going in for that poetry competition at school?"

He laughed, spluttering a bit of chocolate sponge across the table. Fortunately, Mum wasn't looking. "No way," he said. "You know me, I can't put two words together – not if I have to write them down. How about you?"

"I'm having a go and so is Chloe," I said.

Joe just nodded, but Mum came out of her daze and caught my eye, her face all white and tensed up. I realised what I'd done – said the forbidden name of my sister.

Because Joe was there, all Mum did was raise her eyebrows and shake her head.

"What's your poem about?" asked Joe. "Both of you," he added, and I felt Chloe, in the middle of my head, glow with happiness.

Mum gave a confused frown.

I waited for Chloe to go first but she didn't speak, so I said, "Mine's about Garfie, but it's not very good. I'm going to have to do it again."

"Can I hear it?" Joe said.

"I can't remember the words," I lied, trying to stop the stupid first verse uncurling in my head.

"What about you?" Joe asked Chloe.

My sister didn't say a word but I knew her poem would be much better than mine and might even win the competition. What I couldn't work out was how I felt about that.

When Joe had finished his third chunk of chocolate roll, followed by his fourth huge dollop of ice cream, I offered to do the washing-up and Joe volunteered to help. You'd think Mum would have been pleased, especially as it was time for *Coronation Street*. But she said no, she wanted to give the kitchen a good clean-up and it would be easier if we left her to it.

"Shall we take Garfie for a walk?" I suggested to Joe. I wanted to get us out of the house before Mum did something to put him off me for ever.

"OK," said Joe. "But before we go – can I see some of Garfie's other tricks?"

I checked with Chloe, who was coming out of her mood. Yes, she was willing to show Joe the "kill" trick.

"Watch this," I said.

Chloe knelt down beside Garfie and stared hard into his eyes. They held each others' gaze for a few seconds. Then Chloe, in a low, sinister, clenched-fist of a voice, said, "Kill, Garfie!"

Garfie turned in an instant from a placid, easy-going creature into a snarling, growling monster. What's more, his ferocity was directed straight at Joe.

Joe jumped back double-quick.

"Don't worry," I said quietly. "He won't hurt you."

"OK, Garfie," said Chloe in her normal voice.

Garfie stopped snarling, relaxed and became his usual good-natured self, licking Chloe's hand and grinning at Joe as though it had never happened.

"Wow," said Joe. "I can't believe the change in him. He had me scared for a minute."

I stroked the soft fur between Garfie's ears. "He scares everyone when he does that."

"I'm not surprised," said Joe.

"Now watch," I said. I looked Garfie in the eye and said, "Kill, Garfie!" in exactly the same tone of voice as Chloe.

Garfie, with a bored expression, started sniffing at Joe's shoe.

"See what I mean?"

Joe grinned. "I do. Just like with the banana and the chocolate button. It's amazing."

"Isn't it just?"

"So has Garfie ever hurt anyone?" he asked.

"Hardly ever, and he never will, unless Chloe tells him to. He's the gentlest dog in the world."

Joe screwed up his nose. "But even when Chloe said 'kill', he only growled. So if you two were ever in danger, would he be any use?"

"Well, for one thing, his growling could easily scare someone away," I said. "But Chloe has a special word – I don't know what it is. If she says it to Garfie when he's growling – he attacks. Once, a man walked up to us on the street and asked us to get into his car. We didn't, of course. Chloe said the word and Garfie managed to bite the man before he got away."

Joe raised his eyebrows, impressed. "But why don't you know the special word?" he asked.

"There's no point me knowing it, because Garfie wouldn't obey me anyway," I said, though the real reason was that Chloe had always refused to tell me. Even now she was in my head, I still didn't know the word.

Chapter 8

Before Joe came along, I had no idea how pulled to pieces your feelings could be. I know it's all in the pop songs, but until then I'd never really understood what they meant. Now the words boomed out loud and clear.

Garfie bounded ahead as we wandered through the park, picking up the sticks we threw for him and bringing them back to us. Joe and I talked . . . and Chloe joined in.

The sun was setting like a big juicy orange dipping behind the trees. I was relieved to be away from Mum. Joe and I walked so close we could have held hands, though we didn't.

I even heard some birds singing, and I don't usually notice things like that.

"My brother Karl's in prison," said Joe.

I'd known there was something about Karl he hadn't told me. "What did he do?"

"He stole some cars. It was his second offence so they banged him up for two years."

"That's awful."

"He deserved it."

"I meant what he did was awful."

Joe, who had slowed down to tell me about Karl, speeded up again. "He was stupid. Always has been, ever since Dad left home. He's never been out of ⸻ble in all that time."

⸻hy are you different?" I asked.

⸻ of answering my question, Joe said, "It's ⸻ll Karl's not at home now. He'd never get ⸻tu."

⸻'s Stu?"

⸻ mum's boyfriend. He's moving in with Mum ⸻e next week."

"Do you like him?"

"He's OK," said Joe. "I'm glad Mum's got someone

. . . she's been on her own ever since Dad left."

I threw another stick for Garfie and noticed how warm and muggy the air was, as if it was going to rain.

Chloe suddenly said, "No one understands what it's like to lose your body."

I was annoyed at her for changing the subject. I wanted to stop her but I didn't know what to say.

Chloe continued. "No one except me knows what it's like. Even Anna doesn't get it. She thinks she does, but she doesn't. Not being able to go where you want or do anything without your sister there – it's horrible."

Actually, I thought, I understand pretty well. In fact, I reckoned, it was easier in some ways for C than for me. She could get away from me w she wanted, whereas I had no choice in the was stuck with her. I didn't say it, though.

Joe was silent for a few moments. Then, low voice I'd never heard him use before, "Chloe, that must be awful."

"It *is* awful," she said.

"Isn't there anything you can do about it?" Jo asked, his voice still gentle.

"What sort of thing? I can't get my body back – it's all burned up. They did it at the crematorium but Anna wouldn't go."

"That's because they were all trying to make out you were . . ." I couldn't say the last word.

Chloe ignored me. "Anna's body belongs to her," she said. "Even though she shares it with me, it'll never be properly mine."

What happened to Chloe's body is too awful to think about. Mum and Dad told me about her injuries. Later, when the doctors and nurses had put her body back together as best they could, they said I could have a look. I didn't want to, though. Seeing Mum and Dad's faces was more than enough.

"Can't you take turns?" asked Joe, taking the stick from Garfie and flinging it several hundred metres. "With you in charge one day and Anna the next?"

No, I wanted to yell, but I forced it back.

"Anna would never agree to that," said Chloe.

She was right – but it felt unfair. Would *you* agree to that? Would anyone?

"Imagine . . ." said Chloe. "You fall in love with a boy and you haven't any lips to kiss him with."

A little gasp escaped from my mouth but neither of them heard. They were too caught up in each other to notice me.

Everything around us seemed to fall silent. Garfie had disappeared among the trees, the wind had dropped and the birds had stopped singing.

Joe said, "I'd like to kiss you, Chloe."

"You can't," she said, mournful as the last lonely bird of the evening.

They both stopped and of course I had to stop with them, though I wished I could take off, fly over the trees and be a hundred miles away. Can you imagine anything worse than to *feel* your twin sister kissing the boy you love?

Joe's beautiful curving cheek came closer and his mouth touched – so gently – against mine – ours – hers. He was kissing my lips but he was actually kissing Chloe. She was thrilled – I could feel her happiness welling up, expanding inside my – our – body like a huge balloon that would grow and grow, until . . .

Garfie came racing up, thumping his tail. Chloe and Joe were too bound up with their kiss to take any notice, so I reached down and patted Garfie's nose.

That kiss went on *so* long. Garfie had run off again and the sun was below the horizon by the time they came out of it. Joe had a dreamy, faraway look on his face.

I felt a little flicker of happiness for Chloe, like a single candle on a birthday cake. I mean, I'm not a complete monster.

"I love you, Joe," Chloe said.

Joe's face broke into an enormous grin. He seemed to have forgotten all about his missing dad, his brother, his mum's boyfriend and his problems at school. It was all gone, for a few minutes at least. I wished I could feel happy for him, but all I had inside me now was a cold, shivery sickness.

"You OK, Chloe?" asked Joe.

"I'm fine," my sister said. "I feel great."

"You looked ill for a minute. I'm sorry if I . . ."

She smiled and I had that weird sensation I get when she makes her face do something I don't feel, as though I'm a puppet pulled by invisible strings.

"I loved the kiss," Chloe said.

"Me too," said Joe.

They'd forgotten me. As far as the two of them were concerned, I might as well have never existed.

I forced myself back into my own head, pushing Chloe to one side. "It'll be dark soon. We'd better be getting home."

"Sure," said Joe. "Where's Garfie?"

"Garfie – here!" I called, and he came running up again, grinning a bit like Joe a few minutes earlier.

We walked home in silence. Chloe had gone into hiding and Joe, I think, was feeling a bit embarrassed after the kiss. I couldn't bring myself to say a single word. I felt as if a jellyfish had wrapped its tentacles round me and stung every centimetre of my flesh.

Chapter 9

I was dreading school next day. I thought Joe and Chloe would be all close and lovey-dovey after their kiss, but they weren't at all. To my surprise, Joe was extra gentle and thoughtful with *me*, as though I was the one he'd kissed, not my sister. I didn't understand, but I didn't dare ask him why.

Chloe hadn't forgotten their kiss, though. It seemed to have made her bolder than ever. At break she told Joe that we didn't want any more butterfly sessions.

"Hey, steady on," I said, but she took no notice. She'd recently started ignoring a lot of what I said.

Joe frowned, probably feeling a bit hurt. We were sitting on the wall outside the geography block and he'd been telling me a bit more about what it was like when his dad had left home. It was the worst possible moment to change the subject. *And* it was a selfish thing to say, because Chloe knew how much I love the butterfly lessons.

Joe said, "But you're doing really well. You're starting to get the hang of it."

He must have thought it was me speaking. I should have told him it was Chloe, but I felt too sore and angry to explain.

"I'm never going to be very good at butterfly," I said, after a few moments' awkward silence. "I haven't got enough arm muscles."

"Course you have. It's just a matter of building them up."

"Who wants big muscly arms, anyway?" said Chloe.

Joe bit his lip, looking for a moment as though he was going to cry. Did he really enjoy teaching me butterfly so much? Was he afraid of losing me? Or losing Chloe?

I was close to hating my sister at that moment – and I mean *really* hating her, not just feeling annoyed, the way I used to in the old days.

I knew it wouldn't last. But while it did, I couldn't make up my mind whether I liked hating her or not. It was horrible but there was a kind of satisfaction about it – a bit like picking off my scabs when I had chicken pox, years ago.

Chloe said to Joe, "We could do something else together instead of swimming."

"Like what?"

"Like . . . listen to music."

"I haven't got an iPod," said Joe.

"Don't worry – we'll use mine," said Chloe. "You can come round after school tomorrow. Or I could come to your place."

Notice she said "I". No mention of me. Where was I supposed to put myself?

Joe shook his head. "Sorry, I'm not allowed to have people round after school. Not at the moment, anyway. Stu is moving his stuff in this week."

I'd seen Stu in his car when he picked Joe up one day from school. He was a big man with short, shiny fair hair cut across in a straight fringe. I'd taken an instant dislike to him, the way I sometimes do with people, without knowing why.

"Oh well," said Chloe.

I felt a twinge of pleasure followed by a stab of guilt.

Then Lisa Major came strutting past, with her usual scornful expression and a friend hanging onto each arm. She cried out, "You two snogged yet?" so that everyone within fifty metres could hear. Her admirers hooted with laughter.

"Mind your own business," said Joe.

More hoots and coos. Lisa said, "She's a headcase, that one. She thinks her dead sister haunts her body. The ghost of Chloe . . . woo hoo hoo . . ."

This sent her friends into hysterics. While the three of them writhed around in a disgusting giggling mass, Joe and I escaped and headed for the sports block – out of habit, I suppose.

"I'll come and watch *you* swim instead," said Chloe. "I love to watch you move in the water."

Joe blushed. Why had Chloe said that? Didn't she know how easily he got embarrassed? She was in danger of mucking things up once and for all between Joe and me – or between Joe and her, come to that.

Chloe and Joe started to talk about music and, would you believe it, they liked exactly the same stuff? Yuk.

Music is one of the things that my sister and I are completely different about. She's into hip-hop while I like the old kind, even going back as far as Mum's time.

I'd pretended to Joe that I didn't like music much, as I was too embarrassed to tell him what my favourites were. You only admit things like that to people you are *really* close to. And maybe you can never get that close to a boy?

Joe grinned when Chloe mentioned hip-hop. "Thought you didn't like music?" he said.

"That's Anna," said Chloe.

"Oh, right."

"I love music," Chloe went on.

Joe bit his lip and I could tell he felt uncomfortable. Did he realise he was being disloyal to me? He should have – and Chloe should have seen that she was muscling in on us again, and stopped herself.

But she didn't. Soon the two of them were chattering hip-hop, doing silly dances and making each other laugh. As the left-out, jealous feeling wrapped itself round me again, I wanted to scream and run away, but there was no escape. Chloe was in my body and there was nothing I could do.

Chapter 10

Chloe is becoming trouble . . . but I don't know what I'd do without her. She has just rescued me for a third time, and this time it was a lot more serious than a history project or a geography test. I hate to admit it, but I suppose she saved my life – a bit like the day *it* happened, all over again.

I'd made up my mind to start liking hip-hop. It was the only way I could think of to get Joe back from Chloe. They were spending lots of time together now, listening to their stupid music. I had to find a way to break this bond.

Chloe's iPod, with all her favourite songs on it, was in the drawer beside her bed. Next to it was her locket

– the one that matched mine – and her address book. I'd hunted everywhere for her diary – I'd have loved to read it – but I don't think she can ever have written one.

I took her iPod to school, hidden at the bottom of my bag. At the end of the day I walked home slowly, listening to the rhythms and trying my hardest to get into the words and music. If only I could discover what it was about hip-hop that people liked so much. I'd asked Joe, but all he could say was, "You either get it or you don't," which wasn't much help.

I'm usually careful crossing roads – especially since *that* day – but I suppose I must have got really engrossed. Maybe my eyes were half-closed as I focused all my attention on the song. I was trying to make out the words – had the rapper really said what I thought he had?

Then a familiar voice yelled, "Look out, stupid!"

I saw the red car and leapt to one side. No time to think – my legs did it by themselves. Whew! The car screeched to a stop and a purple-faced driver jumped out. My legs gave way and I collapsed onto the kerb.

"Do you want to lose *your* body, too?" cried Chloe, almost as angry as the man.

"No . . ." I was shaking all over now and starting to feel sick.

The driver was about my dad's age, with a bald head and moustache. "Straight out in front of me!" he shouted. "You stupid girl – you're lucky to be alive. Thank God I managed to swerve." He pointed to Chloe's iPod, now in my hand. "They should ban those things, out on the street."

As I sat there on the kerb, *that* morning came back to me. We'd taken a short cut, Chloe and I, because of being in a hurry to get to school. It meant crossing at a place where there was no pedestrian crossing or lollipop lady. That shouldn't have been a problem – we are twelve years old, after all.

But there was a nutter of a lorry driver on the road. It's not just me who thinks that. He's due to be tried in court soon and he'll probably get sent to prison for dangerous driving . . . not that it'll be much help to Chloe.

No one ever actually came out and said it, but I knew Chloe had saved my life by getting between me and the lorry that day.

I pushed the thought to the back of my mind.

Other people had come out of their houses by now to see what the commotion was about. A grey-haired woman sat down on the edge of the pavement beside me and asked if I was OK. Someone else wanted to phone for an ambulance, but I told them I wasn't hurt. The angry man offered to take me home in his car. I said no thanks – I'd been well trained not to accept lifts from strangers and, anyway, I couldn't bear the thought of him speaking to Mum.

I scrambled to my feet, feeling a bit light-headed, my knees still shaky. Pushing the mp3 player deep into my bag, I hurried away from them all.

"Chloe," I whispered . . . but she'd gone away.

Mum was upstairs when I got home. I poured myself a glass of squash and took two digestive biscuits from the tin. No need to tell her about any of this. I'd have to take a chance that no one who knew me had seen what happened.

I wanted to say thank you to Chloe for saving me, but she didn't appear again all that evening and night.

I lay awake a lot of the night, thinking about what happened after the accident – the one with me and Chloe, I mean.

Even before I came round from the anaesthetic, I could tell that something was different. I had this weird dream where Chloe had got inside my head. "Move up. Make room," she kept saying. It was like when we were little and we used to curl up together on the sofa and fall asleep. If I wasn't careful, Chloe would grab all the space.

"Get lost," I said, pushing her away.

But once I'd woken up properly I could feel her there, in the place right in the middle of my head where I sometimes get headaches. She was alive, just as much as she'd ever been – in spite of what Mum, Dad and the doctors were saying.

*

Chloe's poem has turned out to be awesome. It's the kind of thing you'd read in a poetry book.

I knew Miss Tough would love it, and she does. She said, "Wow. That's an excellent poem, Anna."

"You mean Chloe's one?"

"Well, yes." Miss Tough twisted a piece of long hair

round her finger. "Though I thought yours was an interesting attempt."

Hmm. My poem about Garfie was rubbish, as I'd thought.

Miss Tough went back to talking about Chloe's poem. "I love the way it doesn't rhyme much but it has a great rhythm when you read it aloud."

I nodded. Chloe's poem, although very good, was a bit of a cheat in some ways. It started off by describing what it was like to have her own body and run along the beach – but I don't remember Chloe ever doing much running. Apart from her dancing, she's always been lazy.

Verse three had me in it – "my perfect twin", she called me. Perfect? She must have been being sarcastic.

Dad was in it, too, in the days when he and Mum were still together. In fact, Chloe did a clever thing where she sort of mixed up her description of losing her body with the way that Dad moved out. It was hard to tell which of those things you were reading about half the time. It really made you think. She mentioned Garfie in just one line – "my precious golden dog". Notice the "my" . . .

Reading Chloe's poem was like going through every emotion I'd ever had, one after the other, and feeling some new ones for the first time. I tried my hardest not to cry, but a few tears leaked out.

Chloe hasn't shown her poem to Mum and I'm very glad, because I know what would happen. Mum would think I'd written it and accuse me of trying to upset her.

So there is one thing that Chloe and I agree about – Mum must not see this poem. Nor must any of my friends – or my enemies. Though if it wins the competition, I suppose they'll have to.

The next challenge is my birthday. *Our* birthday, Chloe's and mine. In previous years it was something to look forward to, but this year, definitely not. Anything but . . .

Chapter 11

For Mum, of course, our birthday is a very big deal this year, but not in a good way. It will be the first one "without Chloe", as she puts it.

I told Mum again at breakfast time today that Chloe is still here, sharing my body, but she started crying into her cornflakes. "How can you be so heartless, Anna?" she said between sobs. She went on to call me callous, unfeeling and a couple more words I hadn't even heard of.

By this time I felt so guilty I would have agreed to anything. And that's how Mum talked me into having a birthday party.

She picked up the subject as we did the washing-up together this evening. "We must invite lots of your friends," she said. Her face brightened up at the thought. "It's important that we make it a happy occasion, for Chloe's sake. That's what she would have wanted."

I managed not to say, "Why don't you ask Chloe what she wants?" Instead, I said, "But I haven't got lots of friends," which was true.

"Don't be silly, of course you have," said Mum. "What about all those girls who used to come for sleepovers?"

"One or two of them were Chloe's friends. And even the ones that were mine . . . some of them aren't, any more." I thought of Lennie, Jessica and the other friends I no longer had, and my stomach gave a sad little lurch.

Then Mum said something awful. "I was talking to a very nice woman in Tesco the other day. We were both stuck in a queue at the till. She said her daughter was in your year. Now, let me think — what was her name? Lisa, that's it."

There was only one Lisa in our year. My stomach

dropped to my ankles. I put down the casserole dish I was drying because I was afraid of dropping it.

"This woman was very chatty," Mum went on. "She told me Lisa gets a bit lonely sometimes. I thought perhaps we could have her round for tea."

Mum's eyes were shining and I didn't want to say it, but I had to. "Mum – Lisa Major is absolutely awful. She's the biggest bully in the school and I hate her. And she is *not* lonely – she has a gang of girls round her all the time and all the boys fancy her. *And* she drinks *and* she starts fights *and* she steals . . ."

The old Mum would have said she didn't want me mixing with anyone with like that. But this new version didn't even seem to hear. Or if she heard, she didn't believe me. All she did was shake her head, as though Lisa was a poor, downtrodden little creature who nobody loved.

"Did you hear what I said, Mum?"

Looking thoughtful, Mum said, "I kind of half-promised this woman that we'd invite her daughter to tea. Surely you can put up with Lisa for a couple of hours? Stop twisting the tea towel, Anna – you'll make holes in it."

Mum seems to think that I can be friends with absolutely anyone, as long as they are female and approximately my own age. Did things work differently in her day, I sometimes wonder? Or has she just forgotten?

I imagined Lisa Major sitting at our dining table, eating our food. In our living room watching our TV. In our bedroom, picking up my things, Chloe's things . . .

"No! Mum, if Lisa Major steps foot in this house, I'm leaving. I'll run away. I'll go and live with Dad. I'll . . ."

"You'll be lucky if he'll have you," said Mum.

I was still reeling from this when she said, "I tell you what – let's invite Lisa to your party. That way, there'll be plenty of other people around and you needn't talk to her very much if you don't want to."

Desperate by now, I cried, "Mum, she'll throw up! She'll wreck the house. You don't know what she's like . . ."

"Of course she won't throw up. I'm not proposing to supply alcohol to your guests, if that's what you're thinking."

"I don't want alcohol. I just want one or two special friends, that's all. Or maybe just Joe. You liked him when he came to tea. Can't we have him round on his own?"

Mum said, "I think you're rather young to be spending so much time with just one boy." She frowned and added, "I didn't realise you were actually going out with Joe."

I thought of Joe and Chloe's kiss and the hip-hop, and misery surged up inside me. "I'm not – not really. If anything, he's keener on Chloe than he is on me."

"What!?" Mum's voice was almost a shriek.

Suddenly I didn't care. "You heard."

Mum was getting angry now. "Don't use that tone of voice with me, young lady. And don't talk nonsense. I told you at breakfast time – I've had enough of your ridiculous and hurtful remarks about Chloe."

I lost it completely at that point. Boiling over, I banged my plate down on the worktop and cried, "She's here, Mum – she's *here*! She really, truly is. All the time, or most of it. Right beside you. Inside me. The only reason you can't see her is that you just won't look."

"Anna, stop it." The washing-up was forgotten now.

"Mum – I'm not doing it to annoy or upset you. I want you to *see* Chloe and she wants you to see her as well. If you did, you wouldn't feel so bad. You've seen Garfie do his tricks for her, so you *must* believe me . . ."

"Do you treat your dad to this nonsense when he takes you out?"

I thought for a minute. I hadn't seen Dad for about six weeks. He is supposed to pick me up alternate weekends and take me for a meal or something, but he nearly always phones the night before with a pathetic excuse.

"Well, do you?" Mum asked again, rubbing her hands dry on her faded blue velour top.

I stood my ground. "It's not nonsense. I've tried to tell Dad about Chloe once or twice but he just ignores me, if you really want to know."

"Maybe he's got the right idea. What about at school? Do you tell your friends that Chloe haunts you?"

"She doesn't haunt me – she's not a ghost. No, I don't tell my friends. Except for Joe. Joe is all right with Chloe."

"Is he now?"

"Yes, he is." Even to the point of kissing her, I thought. But I didn't say it.

With a flash of comprehension, Mum said, "Is that why Lennie stopped being your friend, because of all this talk about Chloe haunting you?"

I felt myself go red. "Maybe."

Mum shook her head. "You're your own worst enemy, Anna. You'll end up with no friends at all if you're not careful."

"I've got Kelly."

"Little Kelly Gascoigne?"

"Yes. She used to be Chloe's friend, but she's mine now. Kind of." I hadn't told Mum about Kelly mending my costume strap – it might have hurt her feelings.

"That Kelly is a funny little girl," said Mum.

"Stop calling her little. She can't help not being very tall. And she's good at art and she plays the violin and she's really nice. I wouldn't mind inviting her to our party."

Mum winced at the word "our", but I ignored it.

"That's one person, so far," she said.

"No, two. Kelly and Joe."

"I'm not sure about Joe."

"Please, Mum. He's my best friend. You've seen how polite he is."

"All right – Joe and Kelly, then." Mum plunged her hands back into the soapy water. "Now, who else? You must be able to think of some more people."

After ten minutes we had come up, between us, with four other names. That made eight altogether, if you counted Chloe and me and my cousin Leo, who Mum wanted to invite "to keep Joe company", as all the others were girls.

I didn't argue. The main thing was that there was no Lisa Major on the list.

Chapter 12

"How's your boyfriend?" taunted Lisa, yesterday at break.

She had a new piercing in her nose which had got infected and was weeping a pale yellow stream. It looked disgusting and you could almost believe, for once, that she wasn't the most beautiful girl in the class. But the ugliness would only last a few days and then she'd be back to normal, unfortunately.

"I haven't got a boyfriend," I said.

"What a shame! Poor lonely little Anna. Do you know, your mum practically begged my mum to let me come round to your house?" said Lisa. "She said you hadn't any friends, you sad little thing."

Her voice made me want to throw up. I was glad Joe wasn't there to hear it. He was off school for some reason, for the third day in a row.

Kirsten and Poppy giggled along with Lisa. All three of them pointed at me and ran their fingers through their hair to make it go wild and wavy like mine.

I turned to go back into school. "You come anywhere near my house, Lisa Major, and you're in trouble."

"Are you threatening me?" Lisa was suddenly right up close to me, looking down from her extra four centimetres of height. She smelt of bargain-price perfume and her eyeliner was squint. To my surprise she was less scary at that distance – maybe because I could see all her faults.

"I'll set our dog on you," I said, hoping Chloe and Garfie would do their bit.

"You wish," said Lisa.

Chloe suddenly joined in. "If I tell Garfie to attack you, Lisa Major, he will, so you'd better watch it."

Lisa went white with shock for a moment. Had she recognised Chloe's voice, like the day we accused her of cheating? But she soon recovered, gave a sniff and said, "Poor little Anna, all on her own now – no twinnie to hold hands with."

"You're pathetic," I told her.

"Come on," said Kirsten. "Let's leave her alone."

Maybe Lisa realised she'd gone too far, because she let her friends drag her off towards the sports block, no doubt to ogle the boys.

"Thanks, Chloe," I said.

My twin had come to my rescue yet again.

In the afternoon we had English Miss Tough came into the classroom with a big smile on her face.

"Poetry competition results!" she announced, dumping her pile of exercise books on the desk. She caught my eye and my heart began to thump like Garfie's tail.

We'd been allowed two entries each. I'd wanted Chloe's name to go on hers, but Miss Tough refused. "There'll be a few of us judging the competition, not just me," she said. "And some of the other teachers wouldn't understand about Chloe."

I saw her point and agreed to put my name on both.

Miss Tough started with the third prize, which was awarded to Ahmed Khan's older brother, and second prize, which went to a girl I didn't know in another class.

Then she said, "First place – and this is for the whole of the lower school – goes to Anna Henderson."

My heart gave an enormous lurch. There was a gasp all round the class. I could hear Lisa and her friends muttering together, a few rows behind me.

Miss Tough said, "This is a deeply moving poem and I would like to congratulate Anna on her achievement."

It had to be Chloe's poem, of course, not mine.

"You'll get your prize in front of the whole school," Miss Tough told me, after a brief round of clapping. My face broke out in a silly grin – caused by Chloe, who was thrilled.

Later, when no one was looking, Miss Tough gave me a wink to show that she understood it was Chloe's poem, not mine, that had won.

I didn't know how I felt. A bit of me was pleased for Chloe, a bit of me was disappointed for myself, even though I knew my own poem was rubbish, and the bit left over was just confused.

I couldn't help glancing at Lisa. She pulled a face at me and someone nearby gave a nasty little laugh.

"Quiet at the back," said Miss Tough and the noise subsided, though I knew there would be trouble at afternoon break.

And there was, even more than I'd expected. I looked for Kelly but she was nowhere to be seen. Lisa and her gang cornered me by the snack table.

"It's what I call blatant favouritism," Lisa said, in a voice that sounded like a little kid imitating a grown-up.

"Miss Tough said the judging was anonymous," I said, as calmly as I could. "No one knew until afterwards who wrote which poem."

"I know what 'anonymous' means," jeered Lisa, scratching her infected nose.

"Miss Tough felt sorry for you – that's the only reason you won,' said Poppy. "Poor little teacher's pet."

At that moment, Kelly turned up and offered me the apple she'd just bought. I wasn't hungry but I took it. I knew it was her way of siding with me against Lisa and Co.

"Thanks, Kelly," I said.

"Thanks, Kelly," mimicked Lisa in a silly voice. "Though I wouldn't want to eat that apple when it's been in her dirty little hands."

Kelly ignored Lisa's remark – good for her. Lisa and the others lost interest at that point and wandered off. I stood beside Kelly, holding my apple and wishing I didn't have a twin sister who shared my body and wrote embarrassing poems. I wished it so hard that my eyes filled up with tears. And then I started hating myself for feeling like that.

For a few minutes, I actually wanted Chloe to disappear – not just temporarily but forever. My twin sister, who was closer to me than anyone else on earth. I couldn't believe what I was thinking – but I couldn't stop.

"Don't cry," said Kelly.

I bit my bottom lip and sucked my cheeks in, but it was impossible to hold back the tears – such a flood of them had built up.

"They're horrible, those girls . . ." Kelly began.

"I'm OK," I said.

*

Kelly and I have started hanging out together after school on the days Joe has sports practice. "Would you like to come to my party?" I asked her one afternoon.

She gave a little gasp and her face broke into a smile. I felt myself starting to blush – it was embarrassing to have someone want to come to my party so much. But when I thought about it later, I understood. Kelly didn't get asked to many things.

Being friends with Kelly is bringing me in for more horrible comments from Lisa and her gang. Lisa despises Kelly even more than she despises me. But it's worth it, because I've actually started to like Kelly for real.

Maybe with Joe and Kelly at the party my birthday won't be too bad after all?

Chapter 13

"So, what have you been doing with yourself?" Dad asked me as I climbed into the front seat of his shiny new car and fastened the seat belt.

It was the Saturday after the poetry competition results and he'd called to pick me up and take me out for a meal and do some birthday shopping. It was over two months since he'd last turned up.

Mum always gets upset when Dad comes out with his excuses, but I'm not sure how I feel. It hurts that Dad doesn't want to see me, but it's a kind of dull ache that I've got used to. I don't want things between Dad and me to change. If they improve, there's always a chance they'll get worse again, and

I'll feel a sharp new pain instead of the old familiar one.

So when Mum came off the phone on Friday evening and told me that Dad was going to pick me up next day for a pre-birthday treat, I got the nasty kind of butterflies in my stomach, rather than the good ones.

Mum's face wasn't too happy, either. "It's because he's not going to be here on your birthday," she said. "He'll be away on holiday with Nikki."

Her mouth went extra-wide as she said Nikki's name, as though it had a bad taste and she couldn't wait to spit it out.

I was upset that Dad had chosen to go on holiday over my birthday. Work trips are different – he has to go abroad whenever his company tells him. But deliberately booking a holiday at that time . . . it was like I didn't exist.

I could feel Chloe in the middle of my head, hurting too. The combined effect of this and my own hurt made it impossible to speak. Mum hugged me, which was one good thing to come out of it. Since Chloe lost her body, Mum hasn't hugged me anything like as much as she used to, which is the wrong way round when you think about it.

Because of all this, when Dad asked me what I'd been doing with myself, I just said, "Not much," in a flat, sulky voice.

"That's not what I heard," he said, pulling away from the traffic lights into the High Street. "Your mum told me you won a poetry competition."

I looked out of the window. We were passing the burger bar and I knew that Joe sometimes hung around there on Saturday mornings. "Oh, that."

"She said you won't let her see your poem."

"It's not Mum's sort of thing," I said.

Dad hooted at a car that went through the next set of traffic lights on red, blocking us from turning right. He swore, making Chloe and me giggle.

"Is it a sad poem?" Dad asked, when we were on our way again.

"A bit," I said.

Dad didn't reply and we continued on our way. We weren't stopping in town – we were heading for Kettleby, where the shops are better.

It wasn't until we'd found a space in the multi-storey and Dad was looking for money for the machine that he said, "It's good, Anna, that you can express your feelings in a poem."

That gave me a little glow, though I wanted to tell him that the poem was Chloe's, not mine. I longed for Dad to know that Chloe was still with us. He misses her just as much as Mum does, even though he doesn't go on about it and hardly ever cries. Missing Chloe is the reason he left home, I think. If *it* hadn't happened, Dad would still be living with us and would never have started going out with Nikki from his work.

But Mum says that missing Chloe is no excuse for leaving. I know she's right, in a way, but I can see Dad's point of view. The house is so full of memories of Chloe when she still had her body, it's almost unbearable sometimes. Maybe I'd leave too, if I could.

I also know that Dad misses Mum and me, as well as missing Chloe. I don't know how I know that, but I do. I can read Dad's mind a bit sometimes, the way I can Mum's. Having Chloe in my head helps me do it, for some reason.

As we left the multi-storey, Chloe, who usually keeps quiet when Dad's around, said, "Dad, it's horrible."

Dad thought it was me speaking. "What's horrible, pet?"

"Everything. The way everything has changed."

No, no, I thought. *Please* don't start saying things like that . . .

After a moment or two, Dad took my hand – Chloe's hand – and said, "I know," in a quiet voice.

"Please come home, Dad," Chloe said.

I tried not to gasp out loud. This was the worst thing for her to say. My once quiet sister was turning into a real trouble-maker. Was that what losing your body did to you?

I felt Dad tense up and started to feel sorry for him.

Shut up, I told Chloe silently. Not that she took any notice.

"I'm sorry," said Dad.

I opened my mouth to say, "It's OK, Dad," but Chloe got in first.

"You're a mean, selfish pig," she said. "You don't care about Mum and Anna and me. All you care about is that stupid Nikki."

I looked sideways at Dad. We were walking, so it was difficult to see his expression properly, but he looked puzzled – probably because Chloe had said "Anna and me".

I wanted to explain – or at least correct myself – but Chloe went on, "You should see what you've done to Mum. She never stops crying. She hardly ever goes shopping, she stays in her room nearly all the time she's at home and she doesn't cook proper meals any more. She's going crazy and you don't even care."

"Anna! You know I . . ." Dad paused. "Is that really true about your mum?"

"Kind of," I said.

Chloe had exaggerated a bit, but not much. Mum did spend most of her time in her bedroom and it was true she didn't cook many meals. I'd started to worry that she might lose her job, if she treated her customers at the bank the way she treated Chloe and me.

"Oh dear," said Dad. "I hadn't realised things were so bad." He held the door open for me and the noise, warmth and beef-burgery smell of the shopping centre hit us as we walked in.

I waited for Chloe to speak but she didn't, so I said, "Don't worry, Dad. I'm looking after Mum."

"I'm sure you are," he said. "I know you're doing your best, but it's not good for you, having to become the parent."

I hadn't thought of it that way but I realised he was right. Mum and I had kind of swapped places.

"I don't mind," I said.

Chloe butted in. "I *do* mind. It's driving me mental."

"You don't seem sure," said Dad. "Either you don't mind or you do."

"I *don't* mind," I said again.

"I think you do," said Dad. "You're in an impossible situation. I shall have to think what to do." He stopped at the entrance to the food court. "Shall we go and get some lunch?"

In spite of everything, my mouth was watering at the thought of a Chinese meal. I said, "Yes, let's."

"Just bloody well come home!" Chloe yelled as we walked past the coffee bar. Several elderly women looked up and one of them shook her head and frowned at us.

Dad blushed bright red.

"Sorry," I said on Chloe's behalf.

"Let's just find a table," said Dad. "We'll have a civilised conversation once we're sitting down."

I hoped Chloe would get the message, but I could still feel her buzzing angrily inside my head. I was beginning to feel afraid of her. She has a lot of power, when you think about it. She can do or say whatever she likes and I'll get the blame for it.

"Shut up, Chloe," I said under my breath.

"Let's sit by the window," said Dad, heading for a table.

We were quiet, all three of us, until the waitress came round. Dad ordered an espresso for himself, and Chloe, blast her, asked for one too. She knows I hate espressos.

"Your tastes have changed," said Dad. Did he remember, I wondered, that Chloe had started to like espressos just before *it* happened?

"Why shouldn't they?" I said. "I'm thirteen next week."

"So you are," said Dad.

The waitress handed us our menus and left.

Dad said, "Look, Anna, I'm sorry I won't be here for your birthday."

I waited for Chloe to say something. I wouldn't have minded her yelling at Dad over this. But she kept quiet. If anyone was going to make a fuss it would have to be me.

The words wouldn't come, though. I suppose it was because I'd been relying on Chloe. All I could do was pick up my paper napkin and mop my eyes, which were suddenly brimming with tears.

"Hey, what's wrong?" asked Dad.

The people at the next table turned to stare at me.

"It's just the way that . . ." But my throat had clenched up and I couldn't say it.

Dad sighed and handed me his napkin. "Is it because Nikki and I are going away for your birthday? Or is it because of Mum?"

"Both," I said.

"Look, I'm really sorry about the holiday thing," said Dad. "I would never have arranged to be away for your birthday. But it's mine too, of course, just a few days after yours. Nikki booked a surprise trip for her and me and I couldn't very well refuse to go."

"Didn't she know it was my birthday as well?"

Dad frowned. "I'm not sure. I put it on the calendar

but she probably didn't see it. So I suppose it's my fault – I should have told her. I'm sorry, Anna."

The waitress appeared with our coffees. I gazed at the thick black liquid in my cup and felt sick. But Chloe picked it up and took a sip, relishing the bitterness. I tried not to pull a face.

Dad pushed the sugar bowl towards me. I'd have liked some, but Chloe said, "No thanks."

"Are you ready to order your food?" asked the waitress, who was still hovering behind Dad.

"I bet you'd like a chow mein, wouldn't you?" Dad said.

Didn't he remember – chow mein was Chloe's favourite, not mine? I always went for sweet and sour. Or did Dad, for a moment, think that it was Chloe, not me, sitting opposite him? Which, of course, it sort of was.

I said, "No, I'll have chicken balls with sweet and sour sauce."

If Dad realised his mistake, he didn't let on. He ordered his usual beef in black bean, and remembered to ask for fried rice and a couple of spring roll starters.

Although I don't see Dad very often, I get the

feeling that, when I do, he actually enjoys being with me. Unlike Mum. I sometimes think she wishes I was the one who'd lost my body, so she could still have her precious Chloe.

"Will you let me see your poem?" asked Dad as we ate our meal.

"No," said Chloe.

Dad had enough sense to leave it at that.

Chapter 14

"*I* love this," said Chloe, holding up a yellow tunic top covered in sparkling daisies.

I hated it, but I didn't say. Since Chloe has such a hard time of it not having a body of her own, I decided to let her choose our present from Dad. Most of Chloe's clothes are still in our wardrobe but she doesn't get to wear them. I wouldn't mind if she did sometimes, but the one time we tried it, Mum let out a shriek as if she'd seen a ghost.

Of course, it would have been fine if Mum had realised that it wasn't a ghost but her own daughter standing beside her. But instead, she cried, "Anna, how could you?" and burst into tears. I ran upstairs, ripped off Chloe's pink top, screwed it in a ball and hid it in our old toy box under a grubby-faced doll with no arms.

Dad never notices clothes, apart from complaining that our skirts are too short, so we got away with the yellow tunic top.

On our way home we stopped off for a walk in the park. It was strange not to have Garfie with us, but of course he couldn't have come on the shopping trip. I had a feeling that Dad wished he was there, running alongside us.

It had been raining but the sun was out now, making the leaves glisten and the grass smell fresh and spicy. Chloe reached out for Dad's hand and I felt safe and secure for a few minutes, the way I used to.

"Tell me more about Mum," Dad said as we walked towards the lake, which was shimmering light blue in the sun.

"She's heading for a breakdown," said Chloe.

Dad didn't reply but he looked so shocked that I said, "No, she's not as bad as that. But she does get upset if Chloe . . . I mean, if I mention Chloe's name. Or if Garfie does one of the tricks he used to do for Chloe."

"Does he do them for *you*, now?" asked Dad.

I could feel Chloe squirming inside my head, but I said, "Sometimes. Remember, that day just before you left?"

Dad frowned. "I'm not sure. It's all such a blur, those weeks . . ."

"Never mind about Garfie's tricks," said Chloe. "What matters is Mum. She's melting away in front of our eyes. Before long she'll be a puddle on the floor. Please come home, Dad, and sort her out."

Dad gave an enormous sigh and stopped walking. "I can't do that, Anna. You know I can't."

"Why not? You're our dad. You belong to us, not to that stupid Nikki."

I admired Chloe's courage but I was getting scared again of what she might say next. My sister was getting bolder by the minute.

I used to like it in the old days when Chloe behaved badly. It made me look good by comparison and I got a happy, smug little glow, knowing she would get the blame. But it was different now, because I knew that anything Chloe said or did would come down on my head with a crash.

"I'll always be your father," said Dad. "And I love you just as much as ever. You know that, don't you?"

I was about to say, "Yes, I do," and tell Dad I loved him, too, but Chloe got in first. "No, I don't know anything of the sort. If you do love us, it's a funny way to show it, going off and leaving us."

Dad's neck went red, the way it does when he's upset. "I didn't leave *you*, Anna. It was Mum and I — we couldn't stay together. Things were already going wrong, before . . ."

"Before I lost my body," said Chloe.

"What?" said Dad.

"Before I lost my sister," I translated for him.

"Yes, of course — before Chloe . . ." He couldn't say the word.

"Before the accident," I said.

"I'm still here," said Chloe. "I wish you'd open your eyes, Dad — you and Mum and everyone else. I share Anna's body now, but I'm still me. Look — I'm Chloe!" She shouted the last few words, but there was no one else nearby in the park to take any notice.

Except for Dad, who looked — well, knocked for six, as he would say.

I was frightened but excited at the same time. There was a feeling of things coming to a head, about to explode, like the time Mum pricked an enormous blister on my toe. As she brought the sterilised needle closer and closer, I dreaded the pain but couldn't wait for the ballooned-up skin to burst and it all be over.

Dad was holding his head in his hands as though he had the worst headache of his life. "Anna, let me get this right. Are you pretending – for some reason I can't begin to understand – to be your sister?"

"No," said Chloe. "No one's pretending. I *am* Chloe and you can like it or lump it, all of you."

Dad shook his head as though if he did it hard enough Chloe might disappear. I could have told him it wouldn't work. I'd tried it once or twice myself.

"Are these the problems your mum was telling me about? Do you actually believe you *are* Chloe, or something?" He didn't give me a chance to answer but went on, "I'm not surprised Mum is upset, if this is what she has to put up with."

I was so hurt I couldn't speak.

But Chloe said, "Of course Anna doesn't think she's me. Listen, Dad. You grown-ups are always telling us to share. For the first twelve years of our lives it was always, 'Stop fighting, you two – you must learn to share your things.' And now, when we do – when we share the biggest thing of all, Anna's body – you can't get your heads round it."

I loved the way it sounded when these words of Chloe's came out. They bounded across the park like a dog let out of a car.

"I've had enough of this," said Dad. "I'm taking you straight home. And on Monday I'm getting you an appointment with a counsellor or a doctor or someone."

"I already see Mrs Furze after school on Tuesdays," I said.

"Well, it doesn't look as though she's doing you much good. Look, I'm sorry, Anna. I don't want to frighten you, but there's obviously something wrong and the sooner we get it fixed the better."

He made me sound like a broken-down car. The huge lump in my throat stopped me from saying a word.

But Chloe's voice somehow managed to push past it. "Whose fault is it we're in this state?"

I was proud of her.

Dad said, "Are you trying to say that I'm to blame for Chloe's accident?"

"Of course not," said Chloe. "Not for the accident. But it's your fault that Mum can't cope. You're the one who walked out on us."

Dad didn't answer. His neck was redder than ever and he was biting his lip – struggling not to cry?

"You've really done it now," I told Chloe.

I could feel her in her place inside my head – cool, calm and pleased with herself.

Dad said nothing at all as we walked back to the car. He strode out so fast I had to keep breaking into a run.

He unlocked the door and we climbed in, still in silence. The rich, rubbery, new-car smell was over-powering. As we turned into our cul-de-sac, I said, "Are we still going to see a film later on?"

Dad gave a hollow laugh. I'd always wondered what a hollow laugh sounded like and now I knew. It made me want to cry.

I was starting to dread what Mum would say when she saw us both like this. Don't let Dad come into the house, I prayed.

"The sooner we get you home the better," said Dad.

I knew what he meant – the sooner he could get rid of Chloe and me, the better. All he wanted was to escape and get back to Nikki.

He stopped the car at our gate but stayed in his seat.

"Thanks for the present," I remembered to say.

Dad shook his head and sat there, waiting for me to get out. He didn't lean over to kiss me goodbye.

I picked up Chloe's carrier bag and said a very quiet, "Bye, Dad." He didn't even reply.

As we walked up the drive, Chloe and I, I could feel her smugness swelling up, bigger by the second, inside my head.

The house was quiet and I wondered at first if Mum had gone out. She hadn't been expecting me back till eight.

Garfie jumped out of his basket and licked my face – or rather, Chloe's face. I stroked him half-heartedly and he turned away. Chloe had gone back into hiding.

I tiptoed upstairs and found Mum fast asleep on

her bed. I pulled the top cover over her in case she was cold and drifted slowly back downstairs, scratching my fingers against the smooth, waxy surface of the banister, the way I used to when I was little. There was a stain on the carpet halfway down where Chloe had once spilt a bowl of custard she was sneaking up to our room.

I turned on the TV, but there was nothing I wanted to watch. All the things Chloe had said to Dad buzzed round in my head. I pictured him phoning Mum and them talking about me – arranging hospital visits and meetings with special doctors and who knows what else. I imagined Lisa finding out, and her face filled my mind, screwed up in mockery, surrounded by the laughter not just of her friends but of the whole class, Joe and Kelly, too.

"How could you, Chloe?" I asked my twin.

Suddenly she was back. "Dad needed to hear those things," she said. "Specially about how bad Mum is."

"But now he thinks I've gone mental."

"Perhaps he's right."

I couldn't believe she'd said this. "What?"

"Perhaps you're cracking up, like Mum."

"Course I'm not. Though if I do, it'll be your fault."

"My fault?" Chloe paused, long enough to make me wonder if she'd gone away again.

I turned back to the TV, trying to block out the words she'd said.

Then she added, "Listen, Anna. If it wasn't for me you'd be dead. Twice over now."

"No!"

"Yes, you would. The day I lost my body and the day you nearly got hit by that car."

"Chloe, stop it. I don't want to think about that."

"*And* I told you about Lisa cheating in the history project. And I've helped you to deal with her bullying, and I've helped you in tests."

"OK, so you have. Thank you. But . . ."

"But what?" There was another long pause, and this time I felt little prickles of fear creeping up my back.

"You owe me big time, Anna."

"I owe you? What do I owe you? What are you talking about?"

"You know what I mean."

I didn't know, unless . . . could she possibly mean

Joe? "Chloe, go away. I don't want to talk to you any more."

"You mean you don't want me here with you?"

"I didn't mean that. I just meant . . ."

But Chloe had gone silent. She was still there – I could feel her, a thick knot of hurt and anger in the middle of my head.

I flicked the channels on the remote and settled on some programme or other, though I couldn't tell you what it was. All I could think about was my sister. Chloe was becoming impossible to live with, but the thought of her leaving me was as bad as losing my own body.

Chapter 15

Joe was the first one to arrive at my party. He was wearing his normal clothes and hadn't bothered to comb his hair. I didn't mind, but Mum gave him a surprised look.

Joe stared at our new yellow top and his face went red, as if he'd suddenly remembered that you usually got a bit dressed up for parties. I gave him a big grin to show that it didn't matter.

I'd persuaded Mum to let me hire a couple of DVDs – one of them girly and the other an adventure film that the boys would like. Mind you, my cousin Leo is not an adventure film boy – he is musical and goes to a cathedral school where he sings in the choir.

Although Mum had invited him as company for Joe,
I didn't really think they'd get on.

Joe plonked himself on the sofa, rummaged inside
an orange carrier bag and pulled out two presents. He
didn't say why there were two, but I knew. Chloe and
I gave him another big smile. She was back, her usual
cheerful self, as though our conversation with Dad
had never happened. I hoped she'd forgotten all about
me "owing her big time", whatever that was supposed
to mean.

The first present turned out to be a hip-hop CD
by one of Chloe's favourite singers. I was so pleased
for her, I felt tears welling up, but managed to blink
them back.

"Thanks, Joe, it's brilliant," she said.

The second present was a notebook with a soft,
flowery fabric cover and thick, smooth, blank pages
inside.

"It's for your diary, Anna," Joe said. I'd told him
once that I kept one, writing stuff in it most nights.

Chloe and I each kissed one of his cheeks. I noticed
he had some bruises round one eye and a sore place
on his chin.

He beamed and it was a good moment – though spoilt by the arrival of Leo, who, just the opposite of Joe, was dressed up in a weird grey suit as though he was going to a wedding, not a birthday party. I expect it was his mum, Aunt Jen, who made him wear it. She is Dad's sister but not like him at all.

Leo and Joe exchanged hellos, looking like aliens from opposite ends of the universe. Then Leo gave me his present, which turned out to be a very posh fountain pen.

I put a cartridge in the pen and tried it out in my new notebook. We all wrote our signatures, including Chloe (with my left hand) when Leo wasn't looking. I loved the feel of the ink flowing onto the silky paper and almost forgot about my party for a few minutes.

When we'd finished trying out the pen, a silence fell. I couldn't think of a way to get Joe and Leo talking. When you get to thirteen, birthdays are as much about entertaining other people as enjoying yourself. I missed the days of being six or seven and just having fun.

Where was Kelly, I wondered – and where was everyone else? Oh, why couldn't Mum have let me just ask Joe to tea?

Then Leo said, "I'm thirsty," and I remembered I should be offering my guests something to drink. But Joe didn't want anything and Leo said he'd go and get himself a glass of water. I think he wanted to escape.

When he'd gone, Joe said, "How's things?"

I told him a bit about Saturday with Dad and the big upset. "Dad phoned Mum later on and they talked about me for hours."

"Did you hear what they said?"

"I managed to listen behind the door to some of it. There was a lot of stuff about me seeing a new bereavement counsellor."

Joe nodded and made a sympathetic face.

"At least Dad's gone away on holiday now," I said. "So they've stopped talking about me for a while."

I tried not to stare at his bruised face. "Have you been in a fight?" I asked him, mostly as a joke. As far as I knew, Joe never got into fights. I'm sure he could fight if he needed to, but he's not the kind of boy who starts them.

"No," he said. "I fell off my bike, down by the canal."

At that moment Leo came back with his glass of

water, and a few minutes later, Kelly arrived. She was wearing a weird, old-fashioned party dress with a blue tied sash and looked like Alice just out of Wonderland. But I was pleased to see her, especially when she gave me a box of chocolate mints.

Then suddenly Chloe, who'd been very quiet up till then, jumped to her feet. "I'm going to play my new CD," she said, making my mouth grin at Joe. He got up too, and they started to do a silly dance.

Chloe always loved dancing when she had her own body. She wasn't very good at it, but she didn't let that stop her. Since moving in with me, though, she hadn't danced as much. Maybe it was because she knew I hated hip-hop. But here she was, ignoring me completely and having a great time with Joe. I tried to grab myself back from her but she wouldn't let go and we almost fell over, which made her and Joe laugh even more.

Apart from making me dizzy, it gave me that horrible left-out feeling, almost as bad as their kiss in the park.

I wanted to run into the kitchen to get away from them, but Chloe was firmly in control.

I was glad when the doorbell rang and three more people turned up. Two of them, Megan and Suzanne, were twins we knew from primary school. We hadn't seen them since the accident, and I'd been dreading it. What would it be like for Chloe and me to see a pair of twins who both still had bodies of their own? Would it upset Chloe? I tried to read my sister's thoughts as we said hello to Megan and Suzanne, but she wasn't giving anything away.

The twins had fair, curly hair which normally bounced off their cheerful plump faces, but when they first arrived their expressions were heavy and serious. Megan handed me a present looking terrified, as though she expected me to start crying any second.

I said, "Thanks," with a big smile, and their faces relaxed.

They looked even more relieved when they saw it was just a normal party, and both pairs of eyes lit up when they saw good-looking Joe. Garfie remembered the twins from way back and jumped up in excitement, nearly knocking them over, which made everyone laugh.

Soon after that, Mum called us through for the meal. She had managed to cook an enormous lasagne (hurray!) and there was masses for everyone, including Garfie, who had a portion in his bowl as a special treat. Mum had made the top go brown and crunchy the way Chloe loves. I could feel my sister enjoying every mouthful.

The last person, Rowan, who is the daughter of one of Mum's work friends, phoned halfway through the meal to say she had a bad cold and was sorry she couldn't come.

No one said much as we ate our way through the lasagne and then started on the birthday cake, also made by Mum. I hadn't dared to ask for a chocolate cake, Chloe's favourite, but Mum had made a coffee and walnut one, which we both like.

Megan and Suzanne are the sort of people who are never short of words, without being overpowering, if you know what I mean. So, once the food was finished they asked Kelly about her violin and Joe about his swimming and . . . well, you get the idea. They didn't ask me about Chloe, thank goodness, but they mentioned her name once or twice in passing, which was kind of nice.

Joe made everyone laugh, telling funny tales about

his brother's adventures when he was a kid. He didn't mention that Karl was in prison and of course I didn't say anything.

I heaved a big inward sigh of relief. Providing Chloe kept quiet from now on, things would be fine. As long as she and Joe didn't get the chance to dance again or, even worse, have another kiss like the one in the park . . .

We were sitting round the table, giggling about this and that, when there was a loud bang on the front door, followed by a scuffling sound and a peal of laughter. Garfie jumped up and I followed him down the hall.

Her sleek fair hair was newly cut in a style that probably cost a fortune but somehow made her face look much too thin. She had tons of mascara and a splurge of bright pink lipstick that was blurring at the edges. Her purple skirt only just covered her behind and she looked even more of a tart than usual. Yes you've guessed it – waiting on the doorstep was Lisa Major.

Chapter 16

"**W**hat do you want?" I asked in a voice like a cheese-grater.

Lisa gave a big false grin. "It's your birthday, isn't it? I *do* like your yellow top. Nice to see last year's styles are still going strong."

I glared at her.

"We thought we'd come and join your party, didn't we, Poppy?"

Poppy emerged from behind Lisa, giggling nervously. She pushed a small wrapped parcel at me. "Happy birthday!" she said. I'd never heard it sound so insincere.

"Thank you," I said. "But you weren't invited." I

wanted to tell them to go away, but the words wouldn't come.

"Who is it, Anna?" called Mum from the dining room.

"No one," I yelled back.

But Mum was on her way to the door. When she saw Lisa and Poppy she said in a coffee-icing voice, "Hello, girls — what a nice surprise."

"We brought Anna a present," said Lisa.

"That's very kind," said Mum. "Let's see, you wouldn't be Lisa, would you? I thought so . . . you look so much like your mum. And your friend is . . . ?"

"Poppy," said Poppy.

"Well, it's very thoughtful of you both to bring Anna a present. Do come in and have some cake. Lisa, I was chatting to your mum in the supermarket only a few days ago."

"Yes, Mum said she'd seen you," said Lisa.

There was nothing I could do but follow them into the dining room, still clutching my unopened present. My stomach told me that something very bad was about to happen.

*

Lisa and Poppy went gooey-eyed when they saw Joe.

"Hello – didn't expect to see you here," said Lisa in a mocking voice.

Joe didn't answer – just gave them a quick glance and then looked away. I tried to imagine what Dad would say if I showed as much leg as Lisa and as much breast as Poppy.

Poppy turned her charm on Leo, who is not bad-looking for an eleven year old, I suppose. Fortunately, he has zero enthusiasm for girls. It was fun to see Poppy drooling all over him, while he completely ignored her.

Lisa turned her attention to my birthday cake. As she started her second slice, mouth full, she said, "How's your job at the bank, Mrs Henderson?"

For some reason, Mum loves it when anyone asks about her work. I could see her deciding that Lisa and Poppy were very nice girls and would make ideal friends for me. I hate it when Mum gets taken in by people. She is much too trusting for her own good – and mine.

"You haven't opened your present, Anna," said Lisa, swallowing her last mouthful of cake.

So I had to open it in front of everyone, at the table, with Mum beaming at me – and what do you think it was? What would Lisa choose, to give me maximum humiliation? No, not tampons – not even Lisa could get away with that – but it was almost as bad.

Extra-strong underarm deodorant, that's what it was. The stuff that the advert says, "Gets you through those difficult days." In other words, I smelt.

I must have gone as red as a tomato, but all Mum said was, "How very kind of you." She knew it was an embarrassing present, of course, but she'd convinced herself that Lisa and Poppy had made a silly mistake – or perhaps, poor darlings, that they hadn't got enough money to buy me anything better.

"Thank you *very* much," I said in a vinegary voice.

"I'm sure you can find a use for it," said Lisa, sounding like a trickle of strawberry jam.

There was a long silence – even Megan and Suzanne didn't know what to say.

Eventually, Poppy asked, "What are we going to do after the food?"

Before I could tell them it was none of their business because they weren't staying, Mum said,

"We've hired some DVDs. Would you like to stay and watch them with us?"

"Only if it's no trouble," said Lisa.

"Of course it's no trouble," said Mum. "You're very welcome to join the party.'

Had Mum forgotten the deodorant already? Did she really, really not understand what Lisa and Poppy were up to? I had to escape at this point. Pushing past everyone, I headed for the bathroom.

I sat on the loo with the lid down for at least ten minutes, trying to calm down, mopping my hot tears with toilet paper and wondering how I could hide the fact that I'd been crying.

*

Watching the adventure film wasn't too bad. Lisa and Poppy behaved themselves, more or less, though they were sitting one on either side of Joe on the big sofa and they grabbed hold of him every time there was a scary bit. But I saw him wince once or twice, so I wasn't too bothered.

I even started to think that my party might not be ruined after all, especially when Mum brought in microwave-popped popcorn and cans of coke.

But the DVD finished and it was still too early for people to go home. I'd planned to put the girly film on, but Lisa said, "Not that thing, please. I saw it when it first came out and it's rubbish."

We were much too old for party games and no one (except possibly Chloe) wanted to dance. I began to wish everyone would leave, even Joe.

Could I get out of the rest of my party by saying I felt ill? I had the beginnings of a stomach-ache, which may have been caused by too much lasagne, cake and popcorn, or just too much Lisa Major. I was afraid, too, that I might burst out crying any second, this time not hidden away in the bathroom but in front of everyone. It went deeper than humiliation and anger at Lisa and Poppy. There was a sad, dark monster struggling its way up to the surface, and any second now it was going to swallow me whole.

Trust Lisa to find a way to make things even worse. She said, "Why don't you read us your poem, Anna?" She turned to Leo, Megan and Suzanne. "Did you know that Anna won a prize at school for her poem?"

"That's good – well done, Anna" said Suzanne.

"Wow," said Leo in silly voice, pretending to be impressed.

"What was your prize?" asked Megan.

"A book token," I said. "Look, why don't we go and play rounders with Garfie on the lawn?"

Garfie loves rounders. He plays to his own dog rules and it's very funny. But no one wanted to go outside.

"It's nearly dark out there," said Lisa. "Let's hear Anna's poem instead."

Garfie gave a little growl. He could tell I was unhappy.

"Let's have some music," said Joe, looking at me – or rather at Chloe.

"No, no, no – we want the poem," chanted Lisa, with Poppy joining in.

Kelly gave me a sympathetic look but she didn't say anything. Leo was ignoring everyone and playing with Garfie on the floor.

"I want everyone to hear it!" hissed Chloe inside my head. I realised to my horror that any second she was going to start spouting out the words – words that could turn out to be horribly embarrassing. But why, when she knew what Lisa was like? Was Chloe out to make me feel bad for some reason? Or did she feel she wasn't getting enough attention at our party?

"Poetry's boring," said Joe.

Lisa ignored him. "Come on, Anna," she said. "You know you want to, really."

I didn't want to, not one little bit, but I knew I was going to have to. Once again, Chloe was in control.

I opened my mouth to say "no", and the first few words of Chloe's poem came out. I could see as well as hear them – big green letters floating across the room towards Lisa, who put up her hand to catch them and scrunch them up, a look of scorn on her face.

"I'm going to the loo," said Leo, getting up from the floor.

I couldn't stop. I said the next line, too.

I didn't look at anyone as my mouth gabbled the words. I fixed my eyes on Garfie, chewing his rubber bone, and on the flowery pattern on the curtains behind him.

When I got to the end my face was burning.

"What a load of . . ." began Lisa, then collapsed into giggles with Poppy.

"It's a lovely poem," said Suzanne.

"You are clever," said Megan. "But I didn't understand the part about having no body."

"That's because . . ." I started, then realised that I couldn't possibly explain.

"Let's go outside for a bit," said Joe.

"I need to go home soon," said Kelly.

"My dad says people who write poetry are mental." Poppy screwed up her face.

"Then your dad's stupid," said Joe.

"But we all know that Anna's been a headcase ever since her sister's accident," said Lisa.

Several people gasped. I didn't know what I felt any more. Chloe's thoughts had taken over. She was angrier than I'd ever known her – gushing out vile, bitter green stuff that stung the inside of my head. I didn't know whether she was angry because of what Lisa and Poppy said about her poem, or because Lisa had called me a headcase. Maybe it was both.

I put my hand on Garfie's neck. I could feel him growling.

Then a voice, very low, not mine but coming from my mouth, whispered, "Kill, Garfie."

It was followed by the secret word, which I still couldn't make out – and Garfie was off.

Chapter 17

Everything happened too fast to take in. Garfie was across the room, jumping up at Lisa with yelps and barks, and Lisa was yelling. "Ow! He bloody well bit me," and then screaming her head off.

"Down, Garfie," Chloe said. "Over here, now!"

Garfie slunk away from Lisa and came over to Chloe and me, still growling.

Mum rushed in and gave a cry of horror.

Lisa squealed, "Your horrible dog bit me," and held out her finger to reveal a thin line of blood.

Mum went crazy, of course, and started babbling on about tetanus injections and getting Lisa to Casualty, while Poppy prattled on about how her mum was a nurse and if only she was here, she would know what to do.

I looked at Joe and he raised his eyebrows. He understood exactly what had happened.

Chloe, meanwhile, had simmered down and was filling the middle of my head with a warm glow of triumph at what she and Garfie had done.

Lisa's dad arrived soon after, a skinny little man with mean black eyes. He shouted, "That dog should be put down! It's a danger to life and limb." He hugged his daughter as though she'd just been rescued from a pack of wolves, saying, "My poor little princess."

The only good thing was that Joe squeezed my hand in the middle of Mr Major's rant. Or maybe it was Chloe's hand he squeezed, not mine.

Garfie is not going to be put down for biting Lisa, I'm very relieved to say. But Mum had some sharp words with me afterwards.

"You *must* have told him to attack her," she said. "Garfie never, ever bites anyone, only if . . ."

I finished her sentence. "Only if Chloe tells him to."

"He must have thought you were Chloe," said Mum.

Garfie has never mistaken me for Chloe. But there wasn't much point arguing with Mum.

"I don't know what came over you," she went on. "Just because Lisa got you a silly present, there was no need to set Garfie on her."

"It wasn't because of that." I was clearly going to have to take the blame for Chloe – again. "It was because Lisa told me I was a headcase."

"She didn't say that."

"She did, Mum. You weren't there. Ask Leo or Joe or anyone."

"You must have misunderstood. Lisa's a nice girl. I know her mother."

"Just because Mrs Major is nice doesn't mean that Lisa is. And anyway, you've only met Mrs Major once. How do you know whether she's nice or not?"

"I can tell. I'm a good judge of character."

"No, you're not. Not if you think Lisa is a nice girl."

We were going round in circles and I knew, from the way Mum was resting her head on one hand, that she had a headache. I gave up trying to defend myself.

What an end to our thirteenth birthday party.

Mum grounded me for a week, except for taking Garfie for a short walk each evening. But worst of all – can you believe the humiliation of this? – I had to go round to the Majors' house, which was a big, flashy place with a paved front garden full of little empty tubs, ring the doorbell and stand on the doorstep to apologise to Lisa, while Mrs Major, in bright red lipstick and a short skirt that looked like one of Lisa's, hovered in the background pursing her mouth.

Lisa loved every second of it, of course.

The only thing that gave me any comfort as I hurried home, trying to hide my tears from the passers-by, was the memory of Lisa's face, the moment Garfie sank his teeth into her skinny little hand.

Chloe and I had an argument over Garfie biting Lisa. It was only the second proper row we'd had since she lost her body. She was still sore over what Lisa had said about her poem, and I was mad at her for setting Garfie on Lisa and getting me into trouble.

"I thought you'd be pleased he bit her. She deserved it," said Chloe.

"I was pleased, in a way. But it's not fair that I got the blame."

"There's not much I can do about that," said Chloe. "And anyway, I went with you to apologise to Lisa. It was just as bad for me, standing there while she smiled that fake smile and her mum looked at us like dirt."

I wasn't letting her get away with that. "No, it wasn't as bad for you. It was *me* who got into trouble. It's not fair. You interfere with everything I do – you even spoil my party – but no one blames you for anything. You've got it easy, if you ask me. All the fun and none of the hassle."

"That's so unfair!" cried Chloe. Even though I couldn't see her, I knew her eyes were blazing. "How would you like not having a body of your own? Do you think I enjoy having to share yours? And how do you think it feels to be ignored all the time, with everyone thinking I'm not here anymore – even Mum and Dad? You should try it for a while."

"I wish I could. Let's swap over – then you'd see what it's like having to share a body with your horrible boyfriend-stealing sister."

"What?"

"You heard." I didn't care what I said any more.

"Are you accusing me of stealing Joe?"

"I don't need to accuse you – your actions do that," I said, pleased with the way my words came out. "All your dancing to that stupid hip-hop . . ."

"Just 'cos Joe and I have the same taste in music – just because we both like good stuff – you can't blame me for that." Chloe's voice suddenly sounded like Lisa's, so much that I felt hatred bubbling in my stomach, almost as if it was Lisa standing there.

"It was nothing to do with the music," I snapped back. "You just can't bear me to have a boyfriend when you don't. You just have to try and steal him . . ."

"Maybe I don't need to steal him. Maybe he likes *me* best. I'm the one he kissed, after all."

I wanted to hit Chloe, but you can't hit someone who shares your body without hurting yourself. Instead, I screamed, "I hate you! I really, really hate you, Chloe Henderson. You think you can take over my body and do whatever you like –"

"What's going on?"

The bedroom door opened and there stood Mum.

She looked round the room, her face caught up in a frown. "I wondered who you'd got in here. It sounded as though you were having an argument. What on earth were you shouting about?"

"Nothing," I said.

Chloe went quiet, of course.

"Of course it's not nothing. Maybe I should phone Mrs Raj again."

"Who?"

"Your new bereavement counsellor, remember?"

I grunted. "I don't want a new one. I like Mrs Furze."

Mum ignored me. "You've been in a funny mood ever since your party."

"Well, you know why that is," I said.

"It was your own fault, what Garfie did." Mum paused for a minute, then said in a softer voice, "But that's all over with now. You've apologised to Lisa and promised you won't do it again. Why don't you ask Kelly round?"

"Because you've grounded me for a week."

"I'll make an exception – you can have Kelly here for tea."

"I don't want to."

I could tell that Mum was trying her hardest to be nice. I should have been pleased – it was the nearest she'd got to being herself for a long time. But my argument with Chloe was still simmering and I wanted to get back to it. There were a lot more things I needed to say.

Mum took a deep breath. "Anna, shall we go for a walk with Garfie? It's lovely and sunny outside. We could take a picnic to the park."

Now this was a big improvement in Mum and I should have encouraged it. But instead I said, "Mum, go away, please. I want to be on my own."

Her eyes fill up with tears as she shook her head and backed slowly out of the room.

Now I felt both angry with Chloe and guilty for upsetting Mum. I was beginning to feel bad about some of the things I'd said to Chloe, too, especially when she now said, "You're the lucky one, Anna – the one with the body. The one who Mum and Dad still recognise and love."

"They still love you," I muttered. "Much more than they do me. You're still the favourite, just like you always were."

"That's crap, Anna – you know it is."

"No, it's not. You used to be so quiet, Chloe, but now you want all the attention."

"No, I don't. I just want my share of it."

"I hate you! Get out of my body and go away. I never want to see you again."

There was a strange little gasp and I felt something leave me and fly off towards the open window.

I was left with a feeling of emptiness inside my head.

Chapter 18

Chloe has been gone for four days and I miss her like I'd miss one of my arms.

I'm sitting on my top bunk, trying to write my diary, but I can't – I feel too sick. I can't believe I said those awful things to my sister. Worse than anything I ever said when she had her own body – and we had some pretty bad rows back then.

We used to fight over all sorts of things, some of them very silly, looking back. When we were little, it was usually toys. Occasionally, someone bought just one present between us for our birthday or Christmas, expecting us to share. How mean was that? If they couldn't afford two toys, they should have bought us a bag of sweets. It would have saved a lot of hassle – although we sometimes fought over sweets, too.

But the worst rows we had, the ones that made us cry, were always something to do with Mum and Dad and which one of us they loved best.

I was never sure that they loved me as much as they did Chloe. When she was very small, my twin had all sorts of problems learning to talk and walk and run and all the other things most children learn very easily. For some reason, Chloe needed a lot of extra help, whereas I was one of your bog-standard kids who do everything on time.

Because of Chloe's problems, Mum and Dad used to give her a huge amount of praise whenever she achieved anything, however small, while everything I did was taken for granted. Like when I taught myself to swim when I was nine. OK, it's not all that young, but I remember feeling really proud of myself. But Mum just said, "Well done, Anna," before turning back to admire whatever stupid thing Chloe was doing.

When Chloe eventually learned to swim, at the age of eleven – well, you'd have thought she was the first person to land on Mars. They even took her out for a pizza that night to celebrate. Yes, of course they took me with them, but that's not the point.

I'm worried I'm turning into a not very nice person.

Please come back, Chloe. I'm really sorry I said those horrible things. I don't hate you – I love you. You're the closest person to me in the whole world.

Please, please come back.

I've just noticed something strange. Chloe's mobile phone is missing from the top of the little cupboard beside her bed. It normally sits there beside her gold locket, which has a photo of both of us inside it, taken on our tenth birthday. I've got an identical one which I wear under my school uniform.

I've checked the floor and the mattress, but Chloe's phone is nowhere to be found. Could Mum have moved it when she did the dusting?

Or has Chloe taken it with her, wherever she's gone?

Three more days have passed and Chloe is still not back. I've got this awful hollow feeling in my head.

Is this what it's like for everyone else? Is this is how Mum and Dad have been feeling since *it* happened – as though Chloe has gone forever? If so, then I understand them a bit better now.

I'm *so* lonely. It feels as though part of me has been torn off. I've got an arm and a leg missing and half my brain has gone.

At school, I can't concentrate and I keep getting into trouble. At home, I just stay in my room. Garfie knows there's something wrong and he sits on my feet, nuzzling, trying to comfort me. I can tell he's miserable, too. He must be missing Chloe, like the rest of us.

I tried to get him to do the beg-for-a-biscuit trick but he gave me his "you needn't think I'm stupid" look. After that, he licked my hand to show there were no hard feelings.

I wish I could tell Joe about it, but I can't. He hasn't seemed quite as friendly since the party. Like everyone else, he's probably started to think I'm mad.

Lisa is even worse than usual. She has told everyone at school about Garfie biting her finger.

Mum keeps asking what's wrong with me, but she

is the last person I could ever tell. She still cries if I say Chloe's name, so the thought of explaining to her that I'm upset because Chloe has disappeared . . .

But I can't go on like this.

I've just had an idea. I'll try sending Chloe a text message.

No reply from Chloe. It was a stupid idea, I can see that now.

After English yesterday, I stayed behind to speak to Miss Tough. It was one of those times when you know you have to do *something*, however hard it is. I didn't care about being late for history. I didn't care about anything or anyone – except Chloe.

"Is everything all right?" Miss Tough asked me as I hovered by her desk.

"I'm fine," I said, though I felt as if I'd swallowed a rounders ball.

"Did you have a nice birthday?"

I wondered how she knew it was my birthday. Perhaps there is a list of all our dates of birth in the register.

"Not really," I said.

"Was it upsetting?"

"Kind of. Specially when Garfie bit Lisa."

"Ah – I heard something about that. I hadn't realised it happened on your birthday."

"It was at my party. It spoilt everything." I didn't tell her that the party had already been spoilt, before that.

"Oh dear." Miss Tough's face had the tiniest trace of a smile.

"But in the next few days things got even worse," I said.

Miss Tough pulled out a chair for me beside her desk. "What happened?"

I sat down, took a deep breath and told her about my big argument with Chloe.

"You poor thing," said Miss Tough, when I'd finished. "That sounds really awful. And you must be so lonely without her."

"I am. It's eight days now. I miss her so much."

"Of course you do."

For some reason, Miss Tough's reply brought tears to my eyes. I struggled to blink them back.

"Have you told your mum?" she asked.

"No. I can't."

"Why not, Anna?"

"It would make her cry."

Miss Tough gave a huge sigh, as though it was *her* twin sister who had run away.

I said, "I don't know how to get Chloe back."

Miss Tough didn't say anything – she just looked straight at me from behind her desk.

I felt silly and embarrassed, but even more than that, I felt guilty. "It feels like it's all my fault."

Miss Tough was still looking me in the eye. I focused on her sparkly eyeshadow and waited what seemed like forever for her to answer.

"Anna, what happened was not your fault."

"No?"

"No. Definitely not. You are not to blame – not one tiny little bit."

"But I told Chloe I hated her."

"You were angry. We all say things we don't mean at times like that."

"But she's gone."

"Maybe she's not as far away as you think. Could she just be hiding?"

"But why? I've told her I'm sorry."

"Sometimes it takes a while for people to come round."

"I suppose. Chloe always used to go into a big sulk after an argument."

"There you are, then. Perhaps she just needs more time."

A little bubble of hope rose up through my chest and into my throat like a hiccup. "So you don't think she's gone away for ever?"

Miss Tough frowned. "I don't know for sure. I've never come across this kind of thing before."

"Sharing a body, you mean?"

"That's right. So I don't know exactly how it works. But I do know how close you and Chloe always were. I know she loves you. She wouldn't want you to be unhappy, any more than you'd want her to be."

"Course I wouldn't. Not now I've stopped being angry . . ."

"Exactly. And I'm sure Chloe feels just the same. Maybe it'll take her a bit longer, but she'll come round, in her own way."

I felt myself beginning to believe Miss Tough. It

was like having a huge heavy rucksack shifted off my back. I had a short cry – luckily Miss Tough had a box of tissues on her desk. It felt good to have told her about Chloe.

No one, I was glad to see, turned up for the next lesson in that room. Miss Tough must have had a free period. When my crying died down, she said, "Anna, I'm going to speak to your mum on the phone. I'd like to tell her some of the things you've told me."

"It's no good," I said, putting a tissue in my pocket in case I needed it later. "Mum doesn't understand about Chloe."

"Well, no. But she needs to know how upset you are. Maybe it's easier if I have a word than if you try to tell her yourself?"

I felt something inside me crumbling. I wanted Miss Tough to take over, to put everything right. I was old enough to know that she couldn't – not just like that – but I wanted her to try.

"OK," I said.

"Good. Is your mum likely to be at home just now?

Mum was off sick – she hadn't been to work since

the day of my party. "Yes, probably," I said. "But she might be asleep."

"OK. I'll try her in a few minutes. Now, what about you? What do you feel like doing?"

That was a question I'd never been asked by a teacher. All I could think of to say was, "Going to history?"

Miss Tough looked at her watch and then at me. I realised that my face must be red and blotchy and I hoped history would be over.

"They'll be finishing in a few minutes," she said. "It's probably not worth it."

"I could wash my face and go straight to science." Science was the last lesson of the day.

"That sounds like a good plan. If you're sure you'll be all right?"

"I will be." I like science and we were starting a new project on green energy.

"Don't worry about missing history – I'll tell Mr Crewe that I kept you back," said Miss Tough. "And Anna . . ." She hesitated.

"What?"

"About Chloe. I meant to say . . . I have a feeling she's not far away."

Chapter 19

Mum poured me a glass of juice the second I arrived home, and got out the special occasions biscuit tin.

Once, I'd have panicked like mad at the thought of what Miss Tough might say to her, but I'd got to the stage where I didn't really care. If Mum wanted to make a massive fuss then let her. I'd somehow managed to put down the heavy weight of Mum's unhappiness during that conversation with Miss Tough, and no one was going to make me pick it up again.

"I was just speaking to Miss Tough," Mum said in an ordinary voice, neither angry nor sad. She sounded a bit like her old self again.

"Oh yes?" I said through my biscuit. I wasn't giving

anything away until I knew how much Miss Tough had told her.

"She said you got upset in class."

"Not *in* the lesson, after it. And I was only a bit upset." I swallowed half my biscuit whole and nearly choked.

When Mum had finished patting me on the back, she said, "Miss Tough said it was about Chloe."

"Did she say . . . ?" I stopped.

"She said you were missing Chloe terribly and that you blamed yourself."

I didn't reply. Instead I took another biscuit from the tin and gazed at its smooth chocolate surface. Mum had misunderstood, by the sound of it.

"She thinks it might be good for you to see Mrs Raj," she said.

"I'm seeing her anyway, on Friday."

"She thought an extra session might be good. I phoned Mrs Raj straightaway. She's fitting in an extra appointment for you." Mum looked up at the kitchen clock. "I'm taking you in half an hour."

I was aware of the bit of me that should have been angry and upset at this. It reared up just once, then collapsed like an exhausted pony. I didn't have the energy to make a fuss. "OK," I said.

"Look, Anna . . ." said Mum.

"What?" I was still holding my chocolate biscuit, which was starting to melt.

"You know I'm not angry with you, don't you?"

"I never said you were."

"About Chloe, I mean. No one has ever blamed you for what happened. It was that incompetent lorry driver's fault."

"I know it was."

"If I could get my hands on that man . . ." Mum's eyes flashed and her face turned purple, the way it always does when anyone mentions the lorry driver.

"That wouldn't give Chloe her body back," I said.

Mum sighed. "Anna, you know we love you, don't you, Dad and I? We miss Chloe terribly, but we love you just as much as ever."

"I know you do," I said. She wasn't really lying, after all – they'd never loved me as much as Chloe, so nothing had changed.

Mum gave a little sniff. "I'm sorry I haven't been a very good mum recently."

"You're fine. It's OK." I got up from the chair, biscuit still in hand. "I'd better change out of my uniform ready for seeing Mrs Raj."

"Hug?" said Mum, holding out her arms.

I put the biscuit in my mouth and we hugged, but it was more for her sake than mine. The only person I wanted to hug, at that moment, was Chloe.

Seeing Mrs Raj was all right, I suppose. She has three children of her own, who are always up to mischief, and she starts off our sessions by telling me their latest adventures.

"My little girl ate a pound of soft brown sugar yesterday and made herself sick," she said.

It was good, because by the time she'd finished, I was laughing so much I'd forgotten to be nervous.

"You know something?" I said to Mrs Raj, just before we finished.

She turned her big brown eyes on me. "What is it, Anna?"

"I'd like to be a counsellor myself, one day. Do you think I could?"

Mrs Raj's eyebrows went up into her fringe. "I'm

not sure I'd recommend it. You might prefer something less demanding and a bit more fun."

"It's what I want to do," I said, thinking how good it would be to solve someone's problems and make them feel better. Not that Mrs Raj has solved any of my problems yet, but you never know.

I won't go into detail about what she said. I don't remember much of it, to be honest. But the result was, I'm going to see her twice a week from now on.

And I've been given a week off school. Sounds good, doesn't it? But I'm not that happy about it. For one thing, I'll miss loads of lessons and then have to catch up. My science group will leave me behind in the energy project. I won't get to see Joe – and with me away, Lisa will probably close in on him. He doesn't seem to like her much, but you never know. She is irresistible to most boys so she'll probably get him in the end.

Lying in bed last night, I asked myself whether, if I had to choose, I would rather Joe went out with Lisa or with Chloe. It was an impossible question. It struck me that if Chloe has gone forever, then at least I won't have to fight her for Joe.

I turned the idea over in my mind. There were definitely some advantages to not having Chloe around. I shut out the thought – it was too terrible to let myself think it.

Just as I was falling asleep, I thought I heard her whisper my name. But when I said, "Chloe?" there was no reply.

In the middle of the night, I heard my phone beep. But I must have dropped back to sleep before I got the chance to look. When I woke up this morning there were no new messages. It must have been a dream.

*

Mum has decided that she needs to look after me. It's good in some ways. I've been let off all my household chores and she keeps making me my favourite foods. Poor Mum is sick of lasagne, but I'm not. I'd eat it twice a day if I got the chance.

It's not always lasagne, though. We've had takeaway pizza twice so far this week, even though it's expensive.

At breakfast time today, Mum said, "I phoned Dad

and he's promised to pop in and see you on Sunday afternoon."

"What, this Sunday?" I couldn't believe it.

"Yes, why not?"

"But I've only just seen him."

"He wants to see you again. Says he got you an extra birthday present from his holiday."

So Dad thinks he can make up by buying me an extra present, does he? Well, Dad, it's not that simple. I'm still mad at him for being on holiday on my birthday. OK, it was Nikki's fault but he could have said no and got her to cancel it. It's obvious who's more important to him now.

I'm not getting away with doing nothing. Miss Tough phoned Mum to give me some work to do, and Kelly came round after school yesterday to bring me up to date with the science project.

The bad thing is that I haven't seen Joe at all. I keep texting him and trying to phone, but his mobile is switched off. It's probably out of credit or needs charging – that's typical of Joe. I'm doing my best not to mind about it.

I've had two more meetings with Mrs Raj. At the last one she kept going on about death and loss and the grieving process.

"That doesn't apply to me, because Chloe's not dead," I told her.

"However you see it, you're still missing her," said Mrs Raj.

"She's a missing person," I said. "And we can't even send out a search party, because she hasn't got a body to search for."

Mrs Raj just smiled.

*

At half past four in the morning the beep of my phone woke me up. This time, I was determined not to go back to sleep, so I forced my eyes wide open with my fingers, sat up in bed and switched my bedside light on.

Then I read it.

You are such a moron. You think Mum and Dad love me best but it's not true. You have loads more friends than me. And how do you think it felt having

all those exercises to do and everybody laughing
at me in PE?

That was it. There was no "Love Chloe" or "xxx"
at the end.

I read it again, trying to take it in. I'd never thought
that Chloe minded me having more friends. She
always seemed happy to be the quieter one, tagging
along behind.

And I'm sure no one ever laughed at her in PE
lessons. If they did, why didn't she tell me?

I can't work out how I feel about Chloe's message.
It's so good to hear from her, but her words have
given me a horrible stabbing pain in my stomach.

I saved it – I'm *sure* I did – before turning off my light
and going back to sleep. But when I picked up my
phone this morning, Chloe's message had gone.

Chapter 20

Miss Tough has just been to see me at home. It was the weirdest experience, watching from my bedroom window as she walked up the drive. She stopped to sniff at a damp pink rose on the bush that Mum has planted "in memory of Chloe". I don't suppose Miss Tough knew they were Chloe's roses.

She rang the bell and I let her into the kitchen. Her jacket was drenched with rain so I hung it over the back of a chair. Then Garfie bounded up, followed by Mum, who looked a bit flustered.

"Hello, Garfie," said Miss Tough, stroking the top of his head. "What a handsome fellow you are."

She'd met him once before, when she came to see us last October, just after *it* happened.

"What can we do for you, Miss Tough?" asked Mum.

I was about to disappear upstairs when Miss Tough said, "I just popped in to see how your daughter is doing. I thought Anna and I could have a little chat, if that's OK?"

"Of course," said Mum. "Go through to the living room, if you like. Would you like some tea or coffee?"

"Coffee would be lovely, thank you." As she followed me down the hall, Miss Tough said, "How's things, Anna?"

"Not too bad."

"I won't keep you long, but I've had an idea and I want to see what you think."

Once we were sitting down – Miss Tough in Mum's chair and me on the sofa – she said, "I've just heard about a national poetry competition for people under sixteen. I reckon Chloe's poem might stand a chance. What do you think?"

I felt my usual stab of jealousy – but straightaway it was swallowed up by a big wave of sadness.

"I don't know," I said. "It's not up to me – it's Chloe's choice."

"Well, yes. But I thought you might have some idea how she'd feel about it."

"I haven't heard from her. It's nearly two weeks now." I'd decided to say nothing about Chloe's disappearing text message. I was already half-convinced I'd dreamt it.

Miss Tough frowned. "That's a long time for her to stay in a bad mood with you. You've heard nothing at all?"

"I thought I heard her whisper my name one night. Nothing since then."

Mum came in with Miss Tough's coffee, a plate of biscuits and a glass of orange juice for me. She lingered by the empty chair as if she wanted to sit down, but Miss Tough said, "Thank you, Mrs Henderson," in a firm voice and Mum got the message.

When Mum had gone, Miss Tough said, "It may sound a bit silly, but could you perhaps write Chloe a note and leave it somewhere for her to find if she comes to . . . visit?"

I wondered again whether to tell her about the text, but it was too embarrassing. "That's an idea."

"Put it on her bed, perhaps? Does she still have . . . ?" Miss Tough tailed off, her face red, worried that she'd said the wrong thing.

"She still has her bed," I said. "The bottom bunk, below mine. She always had that one, so she could get in and out when she was little. You know, she had to have special exercises to help her learn to walk."

Miss Tough bit her lip. "Of course. Well, Anna, it's up to you, but if I were you I think I'd write a note."

I thought of my new fountain pen and the notebook Joe had bought me. Could I take out a page, I wondered, without spoiling the rest of the book?

"What shall I say – just ask her to come back?"

Miss Tough thought for a few moments. "You could start by saying sorry, to make sure she knows. Remind her how much she means to you."

"I suppose . . ."

"And why don't you mention the poetry competition? My guess, knowing Chloe, is that she'll either love the idea or she'll hate it. Whichever it is, she'll have strong feelings. You might get a reaction from her."

"She might write back, you mean?"

"You never know."

"Or I could send her another text, I suppose. I mean, I could send her a text." Then I remembered that Chloe's phone had disappeared.

"Is her phone still . . . ?"

"It's usually beside her bed, plugged into the charger, in case she ever needs it. But it's been missing for a while now."

Miss Tough took a sip of coffee. "Sometimes a letter can be more personal. I think so, anyway, though people of your age call me old-fashioned. But there's something special about handwriting. Leave it open – don't put it in an envelope."

"What if she ignores it? That would be awful."

Miss Tough had another drink of coffee. "It's a risk, I suppose – but at least you'll have done your best."

I picked up my glass and swallowed some juice. "I bet Chloe *will* want to enter that competition."

"Maybe. But you'll have to wait and see." Miss Tough finished her coffee and put the cup down. "I'll keep my fingers crossed for you. You can tell me what happens when you're back at school on Monday."

"I will."

Getting up to go, Miss Tough said, "Oh, there's something else I wanted to tell you. Lisa Major seems to have hooked up with Tim Reaper. You know, that tall, red-haired boy in Year 10?"

"Tim Reaper? Good G——"

Miss Tough gave a little smile. "I thought you'd be interested."

I wasn't only interested, I was happy – very happy.

"How's Joe?" I asked in a light, airy voice, as though I didn't really care..

"Joe Medway? He's had a couple of days off school himself. He came back covered in bruises – said he'd had a skateboarding accident."

"I didn't know he had a skateboard."

"He looked a bit down, I thought," Miss Tough went on. "I bet he's missing you."

I tried not to smile. Then Miss Tough patted Garfie, picked up her mug and went to say goodbye to Mum.

*

That night before going to bed, I carefully cut a page out of my new notebook and wrote a letter on it to Chloe. I mentioned the poetry competition first, to get her attention. I did it like a newspaper headline, in capital letters with my new pen. "MISS TOUGH THINKS CHLOE HENDERSON IS GOING TO BE A STAR!"

Underneath, I wrote some stuff about how I was sorry for saying I hated her, and how much I loved her. It sounded a bit soppy but I didn't care. It was the sort of thing I'd like her to say to me.

I left the note, as Miss Tough suggested, on Chloe's bed.

In the middle of the night I woke up to my mobile ringing.

I reached for my light switch. For some reason, my heart was thumping with fear. I clicked my phone on and saw Chloe's name on the display.

"Is it you, Chloe?" I said, trying my hardest to sound calm.

After a pause, a little voice said, "Yes, it's me." She

didn't sound quite herself. Something was different – what was it?

"Did you read my note?" I asked.

"Yes, I read it." There was no expression in her voice at all.

"And?"

"I want Miss Tough to put my poem in for the competition."

"Good. And what about the rest of it?" My heart started to thud again.

"The rest?"

Was this really Chloe? It sounded like her, but there was something missing. All her warmth had gone. And she sounded older, that was it – suddenly much older.

"The part where I said sorry for saying I hated you. I didn't mean it. I *don't* want you to go away."

"Right," she said.

That should have reassured me – perhaps. But her voice was still cold and distant, as though she was speaking to someone she hardly knew.

"Really and truly, Chloe, I didn't mean those awful things. Do you believe me?"

There was a long pause. "Yes."

I wasn't convinced. "Please say you forgive me – that we're OK again, you and me."

Chloe's voice rang out with more certainty. "I'll forgive you on one condition, Anna."

"What's that?"

"If you let me have Joe."

"If I . . . ?"

"From now on, he's my boyfriend, not yours. Otherwise . . . well, maybe I'll go away again. Or who knows what I might do?"

From that moment on, it was the worst conversation of my life.

Anna: No, Chloe. You can't have Joe.

Chloe: Yes, I can.

Anna: But he's my friend and I love him.

Chloe: He kissed me. That's more than he's ever done to you.

Anna: That kiss came out of nowhere. You confused

him. And you used my body to kiss him – *my lips*. Can't you see how unfair that is?

Chloe: Why is it unfair?

Anna: Because, unlike you, I can't float away whenever I want. I can't leave you to get on with it while I swan round or whatever you do when you're not with me. Because I'm a normal human being, not a freak who lost her body in an accident and now shares mine. No, not shares, *haunts*. You haunt me, Chloe. You're not only a freak, you're a ghost.

Chloe: You can't hurt me with your stupid words, Anna Henderson. Not any more. Did you really think you frightened me off with what you said? I might have been a weakling when I had my own body, but I'm not now. When it happens to you, you'll discover who you really are. You'll find out, one day.

Anna: Stop it, Chloe. Stop saying those awful things.

Chloe: The trouble with you, Anna, is that you can't face reality. So instead, you keep upsetting Mum by pretending I'm still alive.

Anna: I'm not pretending. You *are* still alive – how could we have this conversation if you weren't?

Chloe: You know the answer to that. I live inside your head.

Anna: Yes, you *live* there. So you are alive.

Chloe: Only in your head . . . in your imagination.

Anna: No – that can't be right. If you were in my imagination, I'd be able to imagine you whenever I want to. I could make you do whatever I want, like making up a story. I could make you be nice to me, the way you used to be. But it's not like that. You come and go just as you please. You ignore me for two weeks, even after I've said sorry. You try to steal my boyfriend –

Chloe: Joe is *not* your boyfriend.

Anna: He nearly is. The nearest I've ever got to having one. We do lots of stuff. We go swimming, or at least we used to . . .

Chloe: That's not very romantic, is it? And by the

way, Joe thinks you're a rubbish swimmer. He told me.

Anna: He did not! When would Joe tell you that? You two have never been together without me.

Chloe: I can whisper to him, same as I do to you. It took me a while to learn, but I can do it to other people now. When I go away from your body, I travel all over the place. I tell people things. I could tell them things you don't want them to know. Lisa Major, for one. What would she say if she knew you hadn't started your periods yet, that you were just pretending you had?

Anna: Chloe – you would never tell her that.

Chloe: Wouldn't I? And what about your taste in music. I'm sure Lisa, Kirsten and Poppy would love to hear about the golden oldies. And Joe too, for that matter. Got into a mess when you tried to pretend you liked hip-hop, didn't you?

Anna: I can't believe you're saying these horrible things. My own twin sister . . .

Chloe: And what if I told Kelly you don't really like her at all – that you just feel sorry for her, having no friends?

Anna: She would never believe you. And anyway, it's a lie – I do like Kelly now. She's my best friend, apart from Joe.

Chloe: But these things are nothing compared to what I could do if I put my mind to it. Do you realise how much power I've got over you? I can do anything I like and you'll get the blame, 'cos no one believes in me. I can wreck all your friendships, spoil things with Miss Tough . . . there's no end to what I can do.

Anna: Miss Tough believes me. She knows you're still here.

Chloe: (*with a weird laugh, as though she's being strangled*) Course she doesn't. She's just pretending, to make you feel better. Mrs Raj is doing the same thing. They know you're a nutter, really. If you're not careful they'll section you into a mental hospital.

Anna: What does "section" mean?

Chloe: You'll soon find out.

Anna: (*nearly choking*) Chloe, what's the matter with you? You've turned into a monster.

Chloe: No worse than those things you said to me.

Anna: I said I was sorry for that.

Chloe: It's too late for sorry.

Anna: I can't believe this, Chloe. Before the accident – we were so close . . .

Chloe: Not always. I sometimes hated you. The way you used to go on about me not having any friends . . .

Anna: I never went on like that. And I never knew you minded, till you told me in that text.

Chloe: You did know! Before last year's birthday party, Mum said, "You can have four friends each." And Little Miss Popular Anna's like, "That means I can have six, 'cos Chloe's only got two friends, hehe."

I never said that. Did I? If I did, it wasn't to hurt Chloe's feelings. I was probably just trying to be funny and wanting to have all my friends round. I'd never meant to be unkind.

I opened my mouth to say sorry, but the line was dead. Chloe had gone.

I leaned out of bed and checked the top of her bedside cupboard. Her phone was still missing.

It was then that the full force of her words hit me. She can say – or do – anything at all, and everyone I know – Mum, Dad, Kelly, Lisa, Miss Tough, Mrs Raj – the whole world, except Garfie and maybe Joe, will think it was me.

And the only way I can stop her is to give up Joe.

Chapter 21

I didn't hear from Chloe again over the weekend, but every time I thought about her I started to shake. I couldn't make my mind up. Part of me wanted her to go away forever . . . the other part wanted her back, more than anything in the world. But it was the old Chloe I wanted back, not the new monster Chloe.

I wanted her beside me, in her own body – as a separate person with a clear space between us.

I wanted to put right all the arguments we'd had. If necessary, I wanted to go wherever she had gone, to meet her in her own place, wherever she lived now.

I wanted . . . well, to be honest, if Chloe really was gone forever, then I wanted to go too.

There – I've said it. The thing you're not allowed to say.

I spent the weekend moping around. On Sunday, when Dad came to visit, I could hardly make myself speak.

"Don't you like your extra present?" he asked.

Of all the things he could have got me, it was a new mobile phone.

I was dreading going back to school, but the Monday turned out better than I expected. When I sat down at my desk, Kelly came over, a big smile on her face, and said, "Welcome back, Anna – I've missed you."

Lisa didn't even give me a glance. She was acting stupid in a corner, with her usual crowd of admirers squealing round her.

At break, I saw Joe on his own at the snack table buying a banana, so I went up and said hello. He looked his usual friendly self. It was hard to imagine Chloe whispering to him, telling him I like Neil Diamond (oops . . .).

Then I noticed that some things about Joe were

different. He had a red spot on his chin, so big it drew your eyes to it, and there was something else not right about his face. I tried my hardest not to stare at him.

"How are you doing?" he asked.

"I'm OK. It's a bit weird, being back at school."

"I know what you mean," he said. "I was off for a few days, too."

I didn't want to let on that I'd seen Miss Tough, so I just said, "Have you been ill?"

He shook his head and offered me a bite of banana. When I said no thanks, he bit off a big chunk himself, before saying, with his mouth full, "Fell off my skateboard. Got a few bruises."

Was that really what was wrong with him? I felt there was something he wasn't telling me. I took another look at his face. His eyes looked sore, that was it – as if he'd been crying. But Joe never cried . . .

"Are things OK at home?" I asked.

"Pretty much," he said. "Stu's moved all his stuff in now. Looks like he's with us for good."

"You don't like him, do you?"

Joe swallowed his mouthful of banana. "I suppose

he's all right. Like I said, Mum loves him, that's the main thing. He makes her happy."

I was going to say that I wished my mum would find someone to make her happy, but Joe changed the subject. Looking down at his sweatshirt, he said, "Look, Anna, I'm sorry, but I can't come swimming this week."

The thought of starting butterfly lessons again with Joe was one of the few things that had made coming back to school bearable. I gawped at him, my mouth hanging open – making me look ugly and stupid, I expect.

"Sorry," he said. "It's just that . . ." He paused and I could tell he was trying to think of an excuse.

"It's OK," I said, though it wasn't.

"This spot," he said, pointing at his chin (as if he needed to). "I'm not supposed to get it wet."

I'd never heard of not getting spots wet before, and I'd had a few myself recently. I wanted to believe Joe, but I couldn't. And it hurt me that he couldn't even be bothered to think up a good excuse.

"No problem," I said, my voice coming out cold and strained, like Chloe's in her middle-of-the-night phone call. "It's not a good week for me, anyway."

"OK," said Joe.

It isn't a good week, as a matter of fact. Two days ago, I started my periods. When I first saw it in my pants, it made me cry. Not because of the blood, but at the thought that Chloe no longer had a body and would never have her own first period.

But it should be over by Wednesday and I'll be OK for swimming. Except that Joe doesn't want to.

"What's up?" he said, and I realised I'd been silent for a long time.

Who do you think popped up at that awkward moment?

"That's OK," Chloe said to Joe. "I've gone off swimming anyway."

What did she mean, gone off it? She'd never liked swimming and Joe knew it. What was going on?

Then I realised. Chloe was pretending to be me. Those threats she'd made – she was making a start on them.

Joe thought it was me speaking. "We could do something else," he said.

"Like what?" I said, trying to squeeze Chloe out of my head.

"I don't know," said Joe. "Listen to music again? Maybe I could come round to your house?"

Ouch! I wanted Joe to come round, of course I did – but I knew very well what kind of music they'd end up listening to. And they'd dance, and heaven knows what else.

"That sounds good," said Chloe, still imitating my voice. "I'd better check with Mum, but I'm sure it will be fine for Wednesday. I'll get her to make lasagne again."

"Yum," was all Joe said.

Then Chloe slipped out of her place in my head and it was Joe and me alone with each other again.

"I've just remembered," I said. "Mum won't let me have anyone round at the moment. She's off sick and she's got to take things easy."

It wasn't true. Mum was back at work and she kept encouraging me to ask my friends round. I'd ended up lying to Joe, all because I was afraid of him and Chloe getting together.

Joe's face sagged with disappointment. I felt sorry for him but there was nothing I could do. The bell rang and we went our separate ways, me to French and Joe to remedial English.

In French I got told off three times for looking out of the window but I didn't care. All that mattered was that Chloe was taking over and I was getting more afraid of her by the minute.

Chapter 22

Had Chloe managed to speak to Lisa, too? Lisa had a great time describing to her band of followers and some other hangers-on how I'd tried to do myself in and Mum had found me unconscious on the bathroom floor. It wasn't true, of course. I don't think many people believed Lisa, but they enjoyed it just the same.

This went on all through Spanish – Mr Davies is not a good teacher – and by the end of the lesson my head was thumping as though someone had kicked it.

On the way to science, Kelly said, "Just ignore them." Like she would have been able to do that . . .

I couldn't even manage to be nice to Kelly. I told

her to mind her own business and she slunk off, probably in tears. Afterwards I didn't even feel guilty.

I walked home from school the long way round, through the park, trying to sort out my thoughts. I'd used my last sanitary pad and the one I had on was soaked through and uncomfortable, but I didn't care. So what if I had a big red stain on the back of my school skirt? The whole world thought I was a crazy freak anyway.

It's not easy to describe what happened next.

I walked up to the edge of the lake and stood there gazing at my own reflection in the calm water. There I was, in my school uniform, my hair a mess. Except . . . my hair was glowing much too bright, almost ginger, and my eyes were green.

"Chloe," I said.

"It should have been you." Her voice was normal, though she looked half-drowned. "Don't you remember, we were walking along and you suddenly caught sight of Lennie and you ran round so she could see you?"

I stared into the water, my heart thumping madly, unable to say a word.

Chloe went on, "Then the lorry came."

It all rushed back. The golden autumn trees by the roadside, the sudden rumble, Chloe's scream, the screech of brakes . . .

The silence. The blood on the road.

Chloe gazed up at me, her eyes full of hate. "It should have been you, not me, who died. If you hadn't run round the other side of me to yell at Lennie . . ."

I did my best to speak, but only a gurgle would come. I tried again. "Sorry."

Chloe shook her head, still staring deep into my eyes. She was disappearing fast, fading away as a duck swam into view, rippling the water. The sun was still shining, way above us somewhere, but I felt like I was wrapped in a clammy freezing fog.

"Sorry's not enough," she said in a faint voice,

"What can I do, then?" My voice was a whisper, too.

"There's only one thing. Give me *your* life, Anna. Your body. Let me take over. Like it should have been, with me alive and you dead."

And with that my sister flung herself at me, clean out of the water, hands outstretched as though to grab me round the neck.

I tried to run – to escape from those clasping hands. I yelled, "No, never! This is *my* body. Go away!"

She wouldn't let go. I was metres away from the lake now but she still had me round the neck, squeezing so hard I couldn't breathe. Squeezing me from the inside, too, crushing my brain, pushing me out.

She was taking over my body.

I struggled against her with every bit of me. I kicked and punched and yelled. It was like one of our fights when we were little, but much, much fiercer. And, unlike back then, I knew I could never win. She was a million times stronger than me.

I could feel my will weakening as her brain took over. A scream shattered my ears – was it her or me?

She must have punched me or something, because I landed on the ground, so hard my breath was all knocked out and my head spun. Her grip relaxed and everything was calm. Not a sound, not even the birds singing.

I opened my eyes. Chloe had gone and I was lying

beside a flowering bush. My knee stung and I saw I'd cut myself on a piece of broken glass.

A woman with a Labrador a bit like Garfie came up to me and said, "Excuse me, dear, are you all right?"

I wasn't sure. Nor was I sure who I was – Anna or Chloe? I tried to think of the special word that makes Garfie attack – the one Chloe knows but I don't.

No word came to mind. I was still Anna.

The woman frowned. "I thought you might be having a fit."

"I'm fine," I said. "I was . . . rehearsing for a school play. I have to fight with a lion." I scrambled to my feet to show her I was OK.

"Are you really sure, my dear? What about that cut on your leg? Perhaps we should call an ambulance?"

I mopped at my bleeding knee with a tissue. "No, I'm fine, honestly."

The woman still looked as though she didn't believe me, so I turned and ran.

Once I'd got well away from her, I slowed down. I walked towards the park gate still shaking, still cold inside in spite of my running and the warm sun.

There was no sign of Chloe.

I didn't understand what had happened, but one thing was clear. Chloe was no longer my friendly twin – she had turned into something else.

Whoever or whatever she'd become, she was a danger to me and I had to get away.

But where? Where could I go to escape from her? She'd gone for now, but she could come back at any time and who knows what she'd do? As well as wrecking my life – school, home, Joe ... she was trying to take over my body.

Somehow, I had to find a place where she would never follow.

Then I had a flash of inspiration – Granny Henderson's.

Granny lives about thirty miles away, in a tiny cottage by the sea. And, more importantly, *she is the only person in the world who likes me better than Chloe.* The reason is that Chloe once called her a "poo". She was only three at the time, but Granny Henderson has a long memory.

I almost forgot my panic for a few minutes, remembering Chloe and me as little kids – all the fun we had chasing each other round the garden, once she'd learned to run. I felt a tear in the corner of my eye, but quickly mopped it up. This was no time for crying – I needed to act fast.

That was what I must do – run away to Granny Henderson's. Not only would I be safe from Chloe but it would be like a holiday. I could paddle in the sea and pick up shells from the beach, just like we used to.

I'd have the spare room all to myself, with the funny old bouncy bed and the thick green eiderdown quilt. Granny would make me apple pie with raisins and a trellis top, and maybe even hot cross buns. And Chloe would never show up. She's been terrified of Granny Henderson ever since Granny came after her with the feather duster that time (Dad went mental).

It would be so good to see Granny Henderson again. I watched the lake from a distance as two swans came in to land and I felt a ripple of happiness. At last, I had a chance to escape from Chloe and the way she had messed up my life.

Then a thought struck me. What if Chloe followed me to Granny Henderson's, pretended to be me and did something awful to get me into trouble with Granny?

I reminded myself that Chloe really does hate Granny Henderson's – the cottage, Granny's cooking, everything. All I could do was hope this would be enough to stop her.

I sat down on a nearby bench to try and think. I started making plans. I would sneak out in the middle of the night and head for the train station. I had some money left over from my birthday, which should be enough to cover the fare. Could I take Garfie, I wondered? No, I wasn't sure about dogs on trains, and anyway, there wouldn't be room for him to stay in Granny Henderson's cottage.

Poor Garfie – he'd think he'd lost us both now, me and Chloe. I pictured his sad, confused face. Then I hardened myself. This was a desperate situation and I had to be strong.

As I made my plans, I felt a new surge of energy and I set off walking again, round the other side of the lake. I was almost cheerful by the time I reached the swans with their cygnet twins, now almost as big as their parents but still grey and fluffy-looking.

Then, for some reason, Joe's face came into my head, the way he'd looked earlier that day, like he'd been crying.

Something clicked inside my head. The reason Joe didn't want to swim. The bruises on his arms and legs that he'd said were from the skateboard accident. His battered face a couple of weeks ago . . .

I wasn't sure, but I had a pretty good idea. It would explain an awful lot.

All of a sudden, I wasn't the centre of my own attention any more. I rummaged in my bag for my mobile phone and pressed Joe's number.

No reply. I sent a text but got nothing back.

Chapter 23

All through teatime, I tried to work out what to do. Could I still run away, now I was so worried about Joe? I didn't want to abandon him, but Chloe-in-the-park had scared me silly and going to Granny Henderson's was such a brilliant plan.

The middle of my head was still empty – no Chloe. But she might be back any time. I had to go – I *had* to get away.

That evening, I tried phoning Joe lots more times. Then finally, just after I'd got into bed, a text arrived from him. "Phone me," was all it said.

Luckily, I had plenty of minutes on my new phone, so I called his number.

"Joe, what's the matter?"

"Hang on, let me find somewhere quiet . . ."

I knew he meant somewhere private, away from the prying ears of Stu.

"OK now," he said a few moments later.

"Joe, what's wrong? I just realised how bad you looked at school. Had you been crying?" Too late, I remembered you didn't ask boys that sort of thing.

"Course not," he said.

"OK. Sorry, I didn't mean it. But you looked kind of . . . upset."

I heard him sigh. After a pause he said, "Things aren't too good here."

"What, with Stu?"

"Yeah. Him and me, we don't really get on. I think he was hoping to get Mum to himself when he moved in. He didn't realise I'd be sitting with them at mealtimes and watching TV. Maybe he thought Mum kept me in a hutch in the garden."

"Oh, Joe . . ."

"He told me to go to my room, just because I changed channels. I wouldn't go and he . . ." There was another pause. "We had a bit of a fight."

"A fight? You mean he hit you?"

"I started it. I kicked his foot. Not hard. Then he . . ."

"He what?"

"Look, I don't really want to talk about it."

"Was your mum there?"

"No. She's on evening shifts this week."

"Did you tell her next morning?"

"Course not. I told her it was a skateboard accident, same as I told you and Miss Tough."

"But Joe – you *have* to tell your mum."

"I can't. She's in love with Stu."

"She can't be in love with someone who beats up her son."

"Not if she knew. But she doesn't know and I don't want her to."

I felt like throwing my phone at the wall. "Joe – you can't just let him do it. He might start beating your mum up, too."

"Calm down, Anna. He wouldn't do that. He loves her."

"It may look like it, but if he gets mad at her . . ."

"He won't. Anyway . . ." After a pause, he went on:

"I did drop a hint to Mum about what Stu did to me. Just a little one. It made me see that she'd never believe me, even if I did tell her."

"She *would* believe you," I said.

"No. Stu is the best thing that's happened to her since . . . well, ever. Probably."

"Tell someone at school, then. Tell Miss Tough."

"No way! No – I'll just have to hope he settles down, once he sees he can't get rid of me."

My brain was starting to work. "Listen, Joe – I've got an idea." And I told him about my plan.

Of course, I didn't tell Joe I was running away from Chloe. He wouldn't have understood, not really, and I could never, ever tell him about Chloe-in-the-park. I told him it was to escape from Lisa Major. That made sense to him, as he'd seen her in action plenty of times.

"But your mum will wonder where you are," he said. "She'll go mental if you disappear in the middle of the night."

"I'm going to phone her as soon as I get to Granny

Henderson's. Mum will only just have woken up by then – she won't have had time to miss me."

This was made up on the spur of the moment, to please Joe. It had never even occurred to me that Mum would be worried – that's how far gone I was.

"Why don't you come with me?" I said. "Granny Henderson won't mind. She'd be pleased I didn't travel on my own. She's always going on about what a dangerous place the world is nowadays. She hardly goes out of her house."

"Hmm," said Joe. "I don't know. What time are you leaving?"

We arranged to meet by the lake in the park at 3:30am next day. From there, we planned to walk to the station, which would take about an hour. There'd be no buses at that time.

Joe reckoned that the first trains left the station at around 5am. He'd got some money – he didn't say where from – and he promised to buy us both a big breakfast at the station café. (Isn't it weird how your brain stops working at times like this? It never occurred to either of us that the café would be closed.)

"Love you, Joe," was the last thing I said before clicking off my phone.

And, would you believe it, he said, "Love you too, Anna."

I felt warm inside, for the first time in ages.

Chapter 24

As Mum kissed me goodnight, she said, "Sleep well, little one."

She hadn't called me "little one" for years and it gave me a strange feeling. It reminded me that she did still love me, in spite of everything, and I felt a bit sad about running away. Not enough to stop me, though.

When she'd gone downstairs I lay there in a sweat, unable to get to sleep, going over our plans.

I'd noticed when I got home from school that Chloe's phone was back on her bedside cupboard. I'd given up trying to understand why it came and went. The fact that it was there, though, meant that she probably wouldn't send me any texts.

But there was nothing to stop her turning up in my head. Did she know what Joe and I were going to do? I didn't think so. It felt as though she was a million miles away, but Chloe could travel at the speed of light and I didn't trust her any more.

Then I remembered the awful Stu, and shuddered under my duvet at what he'd done to Joe.

After an hour or so, I must have drifted off to sleep. The next thing I knew, my alarm was going off – not the gentle music that usually wakes me up in a morning, but a horrible piercing beep. I switched it off and lay there for a few minutes, afraid it might have woken Mum. But there was no sound from her bedroom, along the landing from mine.

As I lay there snug and warm, I longed to go back to sleep. But then I thought of Joe waking up, creeping downstairs and setting off to meet me in the park.

3am and not a whisper from Chloe. She was probably having sweet dreams about Joe, wherever she was. Well, let her dream on. I was taking him somewhere Chloe hated and would never go.

I put on the clean undies I'd left out the night before, my new jeans and a green sweatshirt. Then I squashed a few last-minute things, including a supply of sanitary pads, into my backpack and tiptoed downstairs. Garfie jumped up from his basket in the living room and padded over to lick my hand. I wanted so much to take him with me, and a big lump formed in my throat.

I found a new packet of rich tea biscuits and squeezed it into my backpack along with two cans of diet coke. Joe doesn't like the diet kind but it was all we had. Perhaps he would remember to bring his own drink for the journey. I tried to imagine him getting ready to leave, but I couldn't, not properly. I'd never seen the inside of his house.

At 3:15am I was ready to go. Garfie bounded ahead of me to the door, thinking we were going for a walk.

"Sorry, Garf," I said. "Not this time. Back to bed." He slunk away to his basket and a tear welled in my eye.

I locked the door carefully and was halfway down the path when I remembered Chloe's locket. Even though I was running away from my sister, I wanted her locket with me. Yes, I know – completely mad. Totally irrational, as Dad would say.

So I unlocked the door, worried again that the sound might wake Mum. But all was quiet as I pulled off my trainers and ran upstairs. I gazed for a moment at Chloe's phone, sitting next to her locket on her bedside cupboard.

Then I grabbed the locket, fastened it round my neck next to my own one and hurried back downstairs. Too bad if I'd forgotten anything this time. I knew if I went back now, I'd never leave.

The streets were empty. Lights were on in a few of the houses, but most were in darkness. A dog barked as I passed its gate and I thought sadly of Garfie. Then I remembered Joe, waiting in the park. I was a bit late because of going back for the locket, and he must be wondering where I was. I tried phoning him but there was no reply.

As I got further away from home, I felt myself relax, knowing I was leaving my sister behind.

Sharing a body was not working out. I thought of Mum and Dad, and the evening they announced that he was leaving us for Nikki.

*

Joe and I had agreed to meet among a cluster of trees on the far side of the lake. The idea was to give us cover in case anyone was snooping around. Not that anyone was. The park was even quieter than the streets, and the sudden cry of a duck on the lake made me jump in fright.

3:40am my watch said. I'd brought a tiny torch so I could see the time. When I reached the trees there was no sign of Joe. He'd be here soon, I told myself. I wished I'd put my winter coat on. Although it was late May, my denim jacket wasn't warm enough for the early hours.

A few faint streaks of pink were appearing in the sky, over in the direction of Joe's house. Dawn was breaking already. It would be light, I realised, well before we reached the station. I told myself it wouldn't make any difference to our plan. No one would have missed us by that time; no one would be out looking.

3:55am and still no Joe. I was colder than ever. A whole lot of different birds were singing now. I thought of Garfie's warm body and longed to snuggle up to him. I imagined my bed and wished for a moment I was back in it.

Finally, a rustle in the trees behind me. Joe!

"Hello – you're late," I called.

But it wasn't Joe. A man stood close by, big and scruffy-looking, in an old-fashioned grey overcoat like the one my granddad used to wear. He looked about Dad's age or a bit older, and I soon noticed how bad he smelt – sort of like cow poo mixed with Lisa's horrible cheap scent. Or maybe it was some nasty kind of disinfectant or soap. I crouched back into my space among the trees, hoping he hadn't seen or heard me. But of course he had.

He came closer and smiled when he saw me.

The way he smiled, plus his vile smell, brought the taste of sick to my mouth.

If I'd been scared of Chloe, I was a million times more frightened now. Chloe-in-the-park had been like a dream, although terrifying at the time. This was solid fear – a real live man with a horrible fake smile, who I somehow knew was capable of harming me.

At that moment I wanted to be anywhere other than that place – anywhere else in the world. As long as I live, I will never forget his face – the thick eyebrows, the pale-brown eyes the colour of Garfie's vomit, the ugly, swollen red nose, the blotchy cheeks, the stained teeth, the stubble and that grotesque smile.

For what seemed like an hour, neither of us said a word. Time stopped. I opened my mouth to scream but my throat muscles seized up and my face froze. I couldn't make a sound.

Eventually, he spoke. His voice was high, almost like a woman's. "Rather early in the day, isn't it, for a young girl like you to be out on her own?"

I still couldn't speak. My heart was thumping madly and more sick shot up into my mouth.

He said, "You look cold. Why don't you come back to my house for a nice warm cup of tea? I live very close by."

I found my voice. "No – I have to go home."

He ignored me. "Or a chocolate biscuit or two," he said. "I've got a nice selection of them at my house."

"No . . ."

"I know what little girls like," he added.

His tone of voice as he said those words frightened me even more. All those warnings we'd had from home and school, right from being small. *Don't take sweets from strangers, never get into their cars.* We'd always been so careful, Chloe and I. But now I'd wrecked it all with a mad decision to hang around a park at four o'clock in the morning.

I thought of Joe. Where the hell had he got to? "My friend's going to be here in a minute," I said. "A boy – I mean a man."

The man's eyes scanned the darkness. "I think your boyfriend's stood you up, little miss. Why don't you come with me instead?"

I remembered my mobile phone and fumbled in my bag.

"What's that you're after?" he said.

"Nothing." Where *was* it?

"Is it your phone?"

"No."

"Let me see."

I realised how helpless I was. This man could do anything at all to me. He was looking at me now with an expression that said, Hand it over and I'll be kind to you. Refuse to do what I say and I could be very nasty indeed.

My hand found the solid, comforting shape of my phone, but I had to let him take it. He flung it towards the lake. There was a splash, a bird squawked and it was gone.

Then I started, stupidly, to cry.

"Now, now," said the man, in a mock-kind voice. "I'm not going to hurt you. I've got a cake at home with pink icing. Lots of chocolate bars. Or . . ." He paused, leering at me, his face very close. "Are you old enough for more grown-up pleasures? No, don't be shy. I think you probably are . . ."

"No!" I cried.

"All right, all right." The man looked around, afraid someone might have heard. The sky was getting lighter by the second.

I thought I saw a figure in the distance — was it Joe? But a second later it had gone. Probably my imagination.

The man lowered his voice again, as if he was making a big effort to be reasonable. "I've got a knife," he said. "But the last thing I want is to harm a nice little girl like you. So I suggest that you don't cause any trouble but just come along with me. If anyone sees us, we're father and daughter, out for an early-morning walk."

Anyone less like a father would be impossible to imagine.

He held out a hand to help me up. When I refused, scrambling to my feet on my own, he said, "Don't look so frightened. I won't hurt you, if you do what I say. I used to have a daughter of my own."

Used to? Had he killed his own daughter, then?

He must have seen my horrified expression because he laughed. "Her mother took her to Australia. I miss her a lot. Come on, darling, don't be afraid."

All I could do was follow him, though it was the last thing on earth I wanted to do. Just below my fear, a thought was nagging away at me.

Joe hadn't turned up. Why? Was he in trouble too? Had Stu caught him trying to sneak out? Or had Joe changed his mind about running away? Had he seen sense at the last minute and left me to run into danger on my own?

As I walked alongside the man, I tried not to start thinking what he might be planning to do to me when we got to his house.

Then I couldn't bear it any longer and I let out a sudden enormous scream. It should have rocked the park but it didn't, because it was a silent one.

It was a cry inside my head, to the one person who might be able to help. "Chloe!" I yelled. "Help me, Chloe. Please!"

I still can't believe how quickly it happened. One moment, there was just me and the man, in that eerie early-morning silence, my heart pounding with fear. Then there was the sound of barking – and a familiar golden creature came bounding across the park towards us, tongue hanging out.

Garfie!

And a little voice inside my head, a voice I knew as well as my own, whispered, "Kill, Garfie. Go now, get 'im – *slaughter*!"

Garfie needed no second telling. With a growl, he shot towards the man so hard he knocked him over.

As the man floundered, Garfie sank his teeth deep into his leg.

And only a few minutes later, as the man lay on the ground cursing and swearing, with Garfie standing over him ready to give more of the same, two policemen appeared from around the lake.

Chapter 25

"Another bacon sandwich, Anna?" asked Mum. It was half-past nine in the morning and I was back home, safe in my bed, with Mum and Dad on chairs beside me. I'd eaten a huge breakfast and was starting to feel sleepy. Garfie was lying across my legs – a special treat, as he's not normally allowed upstairs.

We'd spent hours at the police station, where I had to give a statement telling them exactly what the man had said and done. It was horrible, having to live through it all over again.

Everything in my room looked the same as usual, except that Chloe's mobile phone was missing once more from its place on her bedside cupboard.

I'd been trying to work out what had happened. The only explanation that made sense was that my twin had heard my silent scream and done two things. First, she'd opened the back door and let Garfie out of the house. Mum said she found the door wide open when she went downstairs. Second, Chloe had used her mobile phone to call the police, to tell them I was in trouble in the park. It had been a young woman's voice, the policeman said.

Once more, my sister had saved me . . . this time from things too awful to imagine. The policewoman told us that the man was on their wanted list. He'd already been in prison for things he'd done to children, and he was under suspicion for a number of other crimes.

When I thought about what he might have done to me, I couldn't stop crying.

Mum and Dad refused to believe that Chloe had saved me. They concocted a ridiculous story of how I left the door open when I went back for the locket. I'm sure I didn't and, anyway, it doesn't explain very much at all. Why, for instance, didn't Garfie follow me straight out of the house and catch me up on the way to the park?

And who made the phone call? The police traced it to a number which was *one digit different* from Chloe's. How do you explain that? Coincidence, say Mum and Dad. They reckon that someone saw me in trouble and called the police, well before I screamed for Chloe. That would explain how the police got to the park so quickly, which is a bit of a mystery, I suppose. And I did think I saw someone in the distance.

But one digit different – that's too much of a coincidence. I think the police made a mistake and it was actually Chloe who made that call, from her mobile in our bedroom. Maybe she did it even before I screamed – who knows?

All I know is that my sister saved me – and I'll believe that for as long as I live.

*

I spent a lot of the day in tears, on and off, with Mum and Dad beside me. After a while, I found that I was crying not just about the man in the park but about all the other things that had happened. About Chloe, about Dad leaving and about Mum not being herself.

In the breaks between my sobs, I listened to the place in my head that belonged to Chloe. But there was nothing there except my own thoughts. If I stopped thinking, there was just pure silence, very calm and still.

"Thank you, Chloe," I whispered, in case she could hear me.

I must have slept for while after that, because the next thing I remember, Mum was waking me up, saying: "I've just had a phone call from Miss Tough. She's coming round to see you after school."

At the mention of my teacher, I thought of Joe. How could I have forgotten him? Here was I, all safe at home, and where was he? Had Stu attacked him again?

I couldn't even phone him because the man had thrown my mobile into the lake.

"I need to see Joe," I said.

"You need to get some sleep," said Dad. "And I've got to put in an appearance at work and talk to Nikki. But I'll see you again very soon."

"And I'll be downstairs if you need me," said Mum.

As Dad followed her through the door, I said, "Hang on a minute, Dad."

He turned round and came back into the room.

Then I said something really stupid. "Dad, are you coming back to live with us?"

He stopped, turned round and shook his head, gazing at me with big, Garfie-like eyes. "Sorry, pet — no, I'm not. But from now on, you and I are going to spend a lot more time together."

I *so* wished I hadn't asked Dad that, especially when Mum told me off about it later.

"What made you think he was coming back?" she said, her voice sharper than it had been since we got home.

I couldn't explain. I'd felt as though a whole lot of other things had come right, so that one should too. But I could see now that I'd made a big mistake.

"Sorry," I said.

Mum sighed. "Things were already going wrong between Dad and me," she said. "Even before . . ."

"Before Chloe . . ." I began.

"Yes, before Chloe . . ."

I breathed in hard. "Before Chloe was killed on our way to school," I said.

Mum bounded up to me like Garfie. She wrapped me up in her arms and we stayed like that for hours and hours, both crying our hearts out.

Much later, when I'd had another sleep, I called Mum and she ran up to my room. It was good to see her moving fast, like the old days.

"Please can I phone Joe on the house phone?" I asked. "Like I said, he was supposed to meet me in the park. I'm worried about him."

"He probably had the sense to realise what a stupid idea it was," said Mum. "You can phone him this evening. He won't be home from school yet."

Mum was starting to be less upset and more cross with me – much more. I knew I had a lot of telling-off to come.

An hour or so later, the phone rang and Mum brought it to my bedroom. "It's Kelly," she said.

Kelly wanted to know why I hadn't been at school.

"I'll tell you in a minute," I said. "But first of all – has Joe been at school today?"

"You haven't heard?" said Kelly.

"No — what's happened? Is he all right?"

"He's gone away. Miss Tough said he's staying with his aunt and uncle in Hull."

"But why?" Had Joe run away to his own relations instead? If so, he might have let me know . . .

Kelly's voice took on a solemn, important kind of tone. "His mum's boyfriend was beating him up. His mum caught him doing it and called the police. She's gone away too, and her boyfriend has been arrested."

"Bloody . . ." I began.

"I'm not supposed to know," said Kelly. "Miss Tough only told us that Joe's gone to Hull. But my mum's friend works at the police station and she was there last night when they brought the boyfriend in."

I could hardly get the words out. "Is Joe all right?"

"I think so," said Kelly. "I don't really know. I'm surprised he hasn't texted you."

I thought of my phone lying at the bottom of the lake and Joe trying to contact me.

"I do know one more thing," said Kelly. "The boyfriend heard Joe get up in the middle of the night. Joe had got dressed, like he was planning to run away.

The boyfriend hit him and Joe's mum woke up and saw what he'd done."

An enormous wave of happiness knocked me over, so powerful I had to sit down on the bed. Joe hadn't meant to let me down, after all.

And he was safe from Stu.

"Now let me tell you what happened to me," I said.

Chapter 26

"Where *is* Chloe's phone?" Mum asked a bit later, as she put a glass of juice down beside me.

"Haven't a clue," I said.

Mum gave me a look. "That thing about the number being nearly the same as Chloe's . . . it's just a coincidence, you know."

"I know it is." There was no point arguing with Mum.

She gave me another funny look. "I don't want you thinking . . . I mean, I don't want you to be frightened or anything. There's no way Chloe could have . . ."

"I'm not frightened," I said, which was true. I'd been scared of my sister for a while – terrified, especially of Chloe-in-the-park – but I wasn't any more.

"You haven't hidden Chloe's phone, have you?" Mum asked.

"No. Why would I do that?"

"I don't know." Mum gazed at Chloe's bedside table for a few moments. Then she said. "Ah well. Not to worry. Chloe doesn't need it any longer."

"No, she doesn't," I said.

*

"Chloe's gone and I don't think she'll be back," I told Miss Tough. It was a warm, sunny afternoon after school and we were walking round the lake in the park. The water was blue and still, with hardly a ripple. The swans and their twin cygnets gazed at us as we passed.

"How do you feel about that?" asked Miss Tough.

I stopped for a moment while I tried to decide. "I'm OK with it. I don't know why, but I am."

"It was all getting very complicated, by the sound of it," said Miss Tough.

"Yes, it was. Too much to cope with, really. Specially when Chloe tried to steal Joe."

"Did she do that?"

"Yes. She threatened to, anyway. And they kissed."

"Gosh." Miss Tough was lost for words, which was unusual for her.

I decided not to tell her about Chloe-in-the-park. She would never believe me and there didn't seem much point. "It'll be easier now, between me and Joe," I said. "If he ever comes back from Hull."

Miss Tough knew about Stu's arrest. "I think Joe's coming back next week," she said.

'That's good,' I said.

I couldn't let on to Miss Tough that I knew what had happened to Joe. Kelly and I would have to make sure we kept it to ourselves. If Lisa Major and the mob found out, Joe would never hear the end of it.

We were quiet for a few minutes and then Miss Tough asked, "What shall I do about the poetry competition? Do you think we should still enter that poem?"

I noticed that she hadn't called it Chloe's poem any more. Had she ever believed in Chloe, I wondered, or had she just been pretending, the way Chloe had said?

"Chloe's poem, you mean?"

"Yes, Chloe's poem. Do you think she would still want us to enter it in the competition?"

"I'm not sure," I said. A battle was going on in my mind. Did *I* still believe in Chloe? But if Chloe hadn't written that poem, then who had? I'm not capable of writing a poem like that.

"I think she'd still want us to enter it," I said.

Miss Tough smiled. "I'm glad. Because it's an excellent poem. I'm not sure it's good enough to win – there'll be a lot of other high quality ones – but I think it stands a chance."

"Do you think Chloe will write any more poems?" I asked.

There was a long pause. A cold little breeze sprang out of the trees and played around our feet. We were going past the place where the man had threatened me, and we weren't too far from where Chloe and I had had our fight.

"I don't know," said Miss Tough. "What do you think?"

"Maybe she'll write them through me from now on."

Miss Tough watched the swans for a moment. Then she said, "That might work. It might work really well. But would you keep on writing your own kind of things as well?"

"My stories, you mean?"

"Yes, your stories and that diary you mentioned."

"I'm definitely going on with that." I told her how Joe had bought me the beautiful notebook and how I'd been writing my diary in it with my new fountain pen.

"Lovely," she said. "There's nothing like a good pen and some smooth paper to get the creative juices going."

I laughed.

Miss Tough said, "I know Chloe's the better poet, but you are definitely a writer, too."

"It's just a diary," I said. "Anyone can write a diary. My stuff's not special like Chloe's poems."

Miss Tough raised her eyebrows. "If it's anything like your stories, I bet it's pretty good."

I felt embarrassed, so I changed the subject back to Chloe's poems. "If Chloe wins the competition, who gets the credit?"

"That's something you need to think about."

Out of habit, I looked inside my head, into Chloe's place, to ask her. But everything was quiet and still. Not empty exactly – just back to normal. "I don't think she'd mind if I put my name on it. After all, it doesn't matter to her now."

"You could call it Chloe's poem," Miss Tough suggested. "I mean, that could be its title. Then she gets the credit, in a way."

"That's a good idea."

We walked on in silence, the warm sun pressing down gently on our heads.

*

A few weeks have passed since I wrote the bit above. I've filled up my new diary already and am having to write on some old computer printout. Maybe I can persuade Dad to buy me a new notebook on Saturday. He's taking me out for a Chinese lunch and afterwards we're going to call in at his flat. If Nikki and I get on OK, I'll stay for tea. If things don't go so well, Dad and I will go and see a film, just the two of us, instead.

I'm nervous but kind of excited, too.

Chloe has not been back – not since the day she

rescued me in the park. I'm not expecting her to turn up again. That feels sad, but somehow right. The way things were was impossible for both of us.

I'll tell you something, though. In the last few weeks, Chloe has written a couple of poems through me. Really good ones. I showed Miss Tough and she agreed they were Chloe's work. Reading them gives me a golden glow – happy memories of my twin.

It's now the middle of July and the school holidays begin next week. Mum and I have been making plans. We are going to create a garden for Chloe, with her favourite flowers, sweet peas, and her favourite fruit, raspberries. Plenty of other things will grow there, too. It will be my job to keep the soil clear of weeds and to put new plants in every now and then.

Talking of gardens – Mum was tidying up Dad's old vegetable patch the other day and came running inside. "You'll never guess what I've found?"

In her hand, all muddy, was Chloe's phone. It had been missing since the day I ran away.

"Garfie must have buried it," said Mum.

This was hard to believe. "He's never buried anyone's phone before."

"No," said Mum. "But do you remember, when you were younger he sometimes used to bury your toys, as well as hiding them in his bed from time to time?"

It came back to me. "He hid Chloe's toys, not mine." It was another of those things that had made me sad.

"Well, that must be it," said Mum. "I'm glad we've found an explanation for that mystery."

I didn't know what to think. It didn't explain those other times when Chloe's phone had gone missing and then turned up again, all by itself. But there was no point saying this to Mum.

Speaking of Garfie – he now obeys the "Kill, Garfie!" command for me. Joe and I tried it out one day, just to see. Joe agreed to take part, which was very brave of him.

I whispered, "Kill, Garfie!"

Garfie looked surprised for a moment and then started to growl at Joe. I didn't do the next bit, the word "slaughter", which I now know is Garfie's signal to bite. Instead, I called Garfie off, and he stopped growling and relaxed. A look of relief spread over both their faces.

But I know now that if I ever need him to, Garfie will obey my "kill" command.

I've no idea whether Garfie would do the beg-for-a-biscuit trick for me. I don't want to try, because it's not fair on him. I want him to keep Chloe and me separate in his doggie mind. He'll have his own memories of her, and that's the way it should be.

Mum, Dad and I have also arranged a special service at church. It's not a funeral, because Chloe already had one of those last October, the one I refused to go to. This is called a memorial service and it will take place a year to the day since she died.

I can say it now – Chloe died.

It will be very sad and I know I will cry – we all will – but Mum says we should try to make it a happy and hopeful service, too, because that's what Chloe would want.

I suggested, as a bit of a joke, that we played a hip-hop song, and Mum and Dad took me seriously. So Joe will enjoy himself, at least.

Stu is coming up for trial in court and he may be sent to prison. I hope he gets at least ten years. Dad says it won't be as long as that, though.

We're still waiting for the trial date for the lorry driver who killed Chloe.

I've met Joe's mum a few times now and she looks very like Joe – the same dark eyes and long lashes. Fingers crossed she'll find herself a better boyfriend soon. To be honest, I think she's more likely to than Mum – she looks so young and pretty. Though who knows? Mum is looking better these days so she may be in with a chance.

Joe and I are still swimming on Wednesdays and my butterfly is slowly improving. His sentences are no better, though. I'm definitely not cut out to be a teacher.

Something wonderful happened the other day. It was after one of our swimming sessions. I must've looked awful, with my hair all wet and a big new spot on my forehead, but as we walked away from the sports block, Joe said, "You're so lovely, Anna."

"Me?"

"Yes, you." He smiled, showing his perfect white teeth. "Can I kiss you?"

Our lips touched and we had the longest, loveliest kiss you could ever imagine.

My eyes were closed, but in the corner of one of them I could sort of see Chloe. Not Chloe-in-the-park, not Chloe by the roadside, bleeding to death, but the old, happy Chloe with her glowing ginger hair, her beautiful green eyes and her big, wide smile.

She was pleased to see us kissing, I could tell.

THE END

Acknowledgements

I would like to thank the following people for their help with this book:

Emma Langley, my editor at Phoenix Yard Books, for believing in Chloe and helping to make it a better book.

Professor William Yule for his expert advice.

Kay Green, Ann Evans and all my other writing friends, for their inspiration and encouragement.

My daughter, Emily, for being my first reader and providing valuable insight and feedback.

And Paul, as always, for his unflagging faith in me.